Bound by Magic

Irma Koelpin

Contents

Chapter 1

My name is Lilac Reagan, I am 16 years old, I have bright blonde curly long hair with with a really weird eye colour which is different depending on my mood, but as my mood doesn't change that often it is usually bright blue with a hint of brown , and I have a left dimple with a few freckles here and there.

I know it is very weird but I don't mind. So basically I used to live in England, but I am moving to America, Florida to be exact.

At my old school in England I was bullied a lot, and I mean physically as well as verbally.

I don't know why they hatred me so much but I never dared to ask them why so I just let them do what they wanted because in the end I know they just hate theme selves more than me.

"Lilac! We are just about to land!" My mother screeched clearly excited that we are in America, my mum's name is Ria and she has dark blonde hair that reaches to her elbows, and she has bright green eyes.

Don't get me wrong, I am thrilled we are moving here, it's just well a bit too far from home but I'm dealing with it.

"Yay" I say less enthusiastically which made my mum roll her eyes at me while she wakes up my two older brothers, the oldest was 18 years old, his name is Luca (Pronounced Loo-ca) and he has light brown hair with green eyes and a left dimple and he is quite tall.

Riley was 17 and he has dark blonde hair with bright green eyes along with two dimples on both cheeks and a little bit shorter than Luca, and Then there was my youngest sister Willow, she is 10 years old with long straight hair with dark green eyes and quite a few freckles and a right dimple.

Have you noticed we have a lot of dimples in our family for some reason, but I don't ever question it.

"Okay Ria calm down don't get too excited" My dad chuckled still half asleep, my dad is called Rick, and he has brown hair with brown eyes and also a few freckles.

"I know I'm sorry, it's just well we are in AMERICA!" My mum screeched again causing us all to groan, "Shut up, I'm trying to sleep!" Riley groaned again covering his ears closing his eyes again but mum pinched him making him open his eyes, "No fair mum! Not cool!" he said with an annoyed tone.

Mum just rolled her eyes again and put her seat belt back on as we about to land, so with that we all copied her movements and done our seat belts up.

As we landed we got our luggage and went to find our taxi man we hired to get us, "Reagan's family" A man called out who I assume is our taxi man as he said our last name, "Hi we are the Reagan family" My dad said in a polite manner, "We are going to Riverpark Lane number 3363" My mum said as she read the paper of our address, "Yes I know where that is, follow me" the taxi man said as he lead us our of the airport.

We were in the taxi, halfway there so now I was just looking outside and around seeing all the people, "Lilac?" Willow whispered tapping my leg, "Yes Willow?" I ask smiling at her cuteness, "Do you think things will change while we are here?" she asks, "What do you mean?" I ask confused, "Like do you think anything bad will happen again?" Willow said with a clear feeling of worry, "I don't know, but we can only hope" I say trying to cheer her up with a smile which she gladly returned.

We finally arrived at our new house which is quite a modern type house, but it looks really nice, and it is also big!

"Welcome home!" dad said smiling as he looked at the house, "Thanks for the ride here is your money and keep the change" my mum said to the taxi man giving him his money and then we all got out and got our luggage then entered our new house.

As I walked in I noticed there was already furniture which my dad must of brought online, so I decided to go find my room so I walked (More like ran) to my find a nice room but none of them was to my liking so I walked up the last flight of stairs till I was in the attic I think and the room was beautiful, there was a big window at the front and back of the house.

The room was pretty big and it even had a walk in wardrobe and my own bathroom! It is a pretty bit attic, I walked a round a bit more and there was a cute little corner which I have decided will be where will make a comfy place to sit.

"Lilac! Riley! Luca! Willow!" My mum shouted from downstairs, "YEAH!" we all called back from our rooms, "Come down here please!" she called back, so I walked down the stairs where I met my brothers and sister and then we went down the other stairs to the living room where our parents were, "Yes?" I spoke first.

"We will be decorating your rooms soon, so start thinking of what you want your room to look like, and then we will get school set up so when you have your ideas call me or your dad and we will get what you want" My mum said smiling, I looked at them both and smiled back, "YAY Okay!" me and Willow both said in sync which made us look at each other and smile a creepy and disturbing smile, but we failed by laughing.

After our laughing fit we ran to our rooms and I was thinking about how I want my room to be like. After a while of looking around I finally decided so I ran to my mum, "I know what I want my room to look like!" I say jumping up and down smiling.

"Already? Wow okay tell gurl!" my mum said while acting like a teenager, "Okay well I want my walls to be white and I will decorate it with pictures and art as I am a good artist, then I want a double sized bed, with white sheets and polka dot throw with small cute cushions, and then I want a big cushion seat thing I don't know what they are called, but I want one of those and more small different coloured and styled cushions, but I want a unique and antique styled stuff. And I want a light blue carpet with a small fluffy rug, and a fully sized antique mirror. Um a coat stand I don't mind what one just a pretty one, and uh a desk and a antique chest of draws" I say looking at her expression which was actually glued to a piece of paper as she wrote down everything I said and I don't know how she did that.

"Okay nice choices, so basically over all your want is a cute and girly but old fashioned room?" my mum asked, "Yeah basically as long as it is along those lines I'm all good" I smile while I head to the kitchen for some water. As I walked in and got my drink I looked our into our back garden, it is beautiful and we had a built in pool, which is good because I love swimming.

Chapter 2

Late at night:

"Night everyone!" mum said as we all lay in the living room in our sleeping bags watching TV, "Night!" we all said together and soon drifted of to sleep.

Next morning:

I woke up to someone poking me but I knew who it was, "Willow leave me alone" I groan putting my head in my pillow, "No mum said to wake you up the men are here" she said which got me up, "Shit" I said under my breath, "Lilac" Willow warned, "Sorry, don't tell mum I said that" I asked, "Don't worry I wont now get up!" Willow snapped, "Okay okay, I'm up" I say and looked around to see men walking in and out with furniture or just to get more furniture. I got up and put my sleeping bag away then went to find my mum.

"Mum?" I called out, "In here honey!" she called back from the kitchen so that is where I went. "Hey, how long do you think they will be?" I ask, "Um not sure but why don't you go get changed and go out somewhere?" Mum suggested, "Can I come to?" Willow asks, "Yes if you want" she replied, I looked at Willow and smiled so we went to get our clothes and got changed. I got changed into a black tank top, leggings, high tops and a blue jumper. I walked downstairs to see Willow wearing the same as me basically except she had a white top on.

We walked outside as the men kept walking in and out, "Um excuse me?" I said to a man making him look up, "Yes miss?" he asked, "I'm just wondering is there any forests or anywhere, where people don't really go to?" I ask, "Yes there is a forest people do go there but not a lot, so to get there just keep following the road until you get out and then walk right and carry on until you see the forest, you can enter anywhere I think" he said and smiled, "Thankyou and good luck with what you're doing" I smile back then walked away with Willow.

"Are we going to practise?" she asked, "Yupp!" I say popping the 'P', "YAY!" she screeched, I just laughed at her and we carried on walking the directions the man told us.

While walking around I noticed a few shops, "Hey lets get some stuff first" I say and head into a shop, "Okay" Willow replied and followed me.

I brought a bottle of water and some fresh natural sea salt, "Leggo!" I announce and then we carry on walking to the forest.

We finally reached the forest, but I don't think we were allowed in there but we still went in and walked until we were away from the shops so know one could see or hear us.

"Ready?" I ask, "Yeah" Willow replied.

We held hands and made a circle, "What should we do?" Willow asks, "Something simple" I answer, so I thought for a bit, "A wind spell?" Willow suggested, "Yes!" I smile "Okay stay here" I say and walk away to get the big container of salt, and with that I made a perfect circle around me and Willow.

"Okay now think that we are one, and we are the only one with power, think of the wind and how you want only us to be able to feel it" I say, "Okay" she replied.

"Ready?" I say through our mind link,

"Yeah" She replied, so we both started to breathe, I can feel her connecting her power with mine, and together we made the leaves slowly move around, and soon the wind picked up making the trees and our hair and everything fly around, I smiled at our power.

As we finished we just laughed, "God it feels good to use magic!" she sighs, "I know but we have to be discreate" I say sighing as well.

"I think we should go it is getting quite late" I said feeling sad, "Yeah okay let's go" Willow replied.

Okay so if you haven't already guessed I am a witch, and so is Willow, because it runs through our family but the girls side, so my dad and brothers aren't, but my great grandma was and so was our great great great grandma, so basically there is a lot of boys in our family and luckily our generation had 2, me and Willow.

As we walked home we passed some teenagers around my age at a shop, "Hey can I quickly get a drink?" Willow asks, "No can't you wait till we get home?" I ask, "No mum won't let me have anything fizzy" she complained, "Fine" I say rolling my eyes and we entered the shop. "Go get you drink" I order which she then quickly went to get one so I just stood my the door waiting so I could pay for it.

"Hey" Some boy said to me smiling, "Yeah?" I ask not really wanting to speak to anyone right now, "I havent seen you around here before" he smirked, "Mhm" I answered looking for Willow who still isn't back.

"So what's you're name?" he asked, "Go away" I snap which he must of been a bit taken back, "Well hello miss Snappy, but a first name would be nice" he said again, "Lilac?" Willow asked, "Here is my drink" she said smiling so I pushed past the boy and went to pay for the drink and as I did that I gave it back to Willow and we went to leave but the boy stopped me, "I hope to see you again. Lilac" he smiled but I just glared at him then walked away with Willow.

"Who was that?" she asked, "Okay we have been here for like a day, so seriosuly how the hell should I know?" I ask looking at her, which she shrugged back, "I don't know" she said, "Exactly" I smile as we walk back home and finally arrived back to find that all the men were now gone so I'm guessing they have finished.

"Mum, we're home!" I call out looking around to see our perfectly finished house, "HERE!" mum called out from the kitchen so me and Willow walked to the kitchen to see everyone at the table while mum starts to put food on the plates. "Hellooo" I said while sitting down, "Hey girls, how was you're day?" mum asked, "Good" me and Willow both replied smiling at each other, "Good, okay so now that all our rooms are done, you will all be starting school in 2 days okay?" dad said which made us all groan annoyed, "Okay now dig in!" mum said as she finished placing our food on our plates, so with that we all ate.

Chapter 3

Two days later:

My alarm woke me up at 6:30am I groaned but got up and took a quick shower, and as I got out I went to my walk in wardrobe and decided to wear light ripped blue jeans and a guns n roses top with my red jacket and black vans.

I did a little makeup which was just mascara and a little eye liner, then I just left my hair in it's natural curliness.

I walked downstairs to see everyone having breakfast, "Morning" I said but know one heard me as I was really tired so my voice was quiet but Luca noticed "Morning" he replied smiling, which made everyone else notice me and say morning.

I sat down and ate some cereal and a cup of tea, "Okay what time do we need to be at school?" Riley asked, "Um 9:00, so I will drop you of in a bit, oh and Luca, your dad is getting you a car so you will be driving to school tomorrow and you can take everyone else while I take Willow okay?" mum asked, "Sure" Riley said while stuffing his face with food smiling at the fact he will have a new car.

As I finished brushing my teeth I walked outside to meet my mum in the car along with everyone else, so I sat in the back and we soon left for school.

As we arrived I said bye and left to go get my time table along with Riley and Luca.

We walked until we found a lady at a desk which I guess is registration, so we walked up to her, "Excuse me?" I started making the lady look up at us and smile, "Hi, I'm Lilac, this is Luca and Riley we are new here" I said, "Oh yes okay hold on let me get you're time tables" she smiled and got up to get what she was getting.

As the lady returned she sat back down, "Lilac Reagan?" She asked to make sure I was her, "Yes that's me" I smile while she hands me my time table, and she gave the others to Riley and Luca.

"What do you all have first?" Luca asks, "I have Maths" I say, "ICT" Riley also said, "I have English" Luca groaned, "Okay well go to our first lessons, and well yeah let's just go" I said smiling, "Okay see you in a bit" Riley said, "Yeah see ya" Luca replied, "Bye" I said and gave them a quick hug before heading towards maths, which I found easier than I should of but oh well.

As I entered my maths class everyone was staring at me, "Hi sorry I'm late, I got a bit lost" I lie as really I was busy with my brothers, "Oh yes hi, I'm Miss Bree, and you're Lilac right?" she said, "Yeah" I replied, "Nice to meet you" she stated until she started to talk to the class, "Okay everyone this is Lilac Reagan, she moved here from England, and I would like you to be kind to her please" she said as everyone nodded still staring at me which made me feel uncomfortable, "Okay well you can sit over there" she pointed to an empty seat by the window, "Okay thanks" I reply smiling making my way over with everyone still staring at me.

I sat down and looked out to the window, "Lilac here is you're new book" Miss said smiling while handing me my book, "Thanks" I reply while writing the information needed then started to do what the teacher was doing which was algebra, and I LOVE algebra!

I was ahead of the class, as before I left school in England we were also doing algebra so I knew what I was doing, where as this class have only just started so I know what I'm on about.

"How are you doing so far?" Miss Bree asked, "I'm done" I reply which made her look shocked, "Wow, okay let me check the answers" she said while checking them so I looked back out the window seeing all the trees and the nature, it just made me feel happy.

"Well done, they are all right" she smiled, "Yeah in England we were doing algebra so yeah" I smile back, "Okay well class will be finished in a bit so you can just sit down and relax a bit" miss said so with that she walked of.

I looked outside again and started to want the trees to move their branches, and while thinking that the branches moved around a bit fast which made me smile.

"Um, hey" a voice said next to me, so I quickly looked who was there and a girl was there.

"Hi, I'm Leanne, you're Lilac right?" she said, "Yeah?" I answered a bit confused why she was next to me, "So how are you?" she asked trying to make conversation, "Fine, you?" I asked back, "Good" she answered clearly feeling a bit awkward.

"What do you have next?" she asked, "Um I think I have free period" I answered, "Me too!" she squealed.

"You will come with me and I will introduce you to my friends is that okay?" she asked, "Sure?" I answered making it sound more of a question but she still smiled.

As the bell went I got my stuff and was dragged away by Leanne, I laughed at her eagerness.

"Hey guys!" she smiled at all her friends that were outside near some benches, "Hey" they all replied in sync.

"This is Lilac" she introduced me which made everyone look at me, "Hi" I said not really knowing what to say.

"Lilac!" the boy from the shop said as he approached me, "Nice to see you again" he smiled, "Um okay?" I said confused.

"Oh yeah Im Nick" he smiled offering me his hand which I shook, "So you go to this school then?" he asked, "Well no shit Sherlock" I scoffed which made him smirk, "Oh yeah, sorry I guess I'm just having a blonde moment" he laughed making me laugh a little.

"Okay so this is Louise" Leanne introduced her friends, "And this is Louis, and then it's Mike, then Chloe, then Jade, then Tommo, and you know Nick, and there are more but they don't have free period so we will see them at break" Leanne smiled, "Okay" I answered smiling back.

I can tell she is part of the popular group which I don't mind, I was actually happy because I'm not being bullied for once.

"Okay so Lilac" Louise started, "Yes?" I dragged the 'S' "What is it like in England?" she asked, "Cold" I simply replied with a smirk and that made her giggle, "True, well I've never been there but people say it is cold" she laughs, "Very" I reply with a serious tone.

"Okay next question, why did you move here?" she asked, "Well things were happening back at England so we decided to move away and well my dad always wanted to live in America and so did my mum so they picked this place" I answered trying to avoid the reason why we left.

"Oooooooohh" she replied nodding her head slowly, I just smiled, "So is there anything I need to know about this school?" I ask.

"YES!" Louise and Leanne both replied at the same time smiling at each other.

"Okay first, our school are like serious with the whole clicks, and stuff, so I suppose we should start with that" Leanne started.

"Go on" I say for her to carry on, "Well there is our group, the popular as some call us, and then there are the obvious ones, but the ones we socialize with are these two groups in particular, which is what we call Hotties 1 and Hotties 2" Louise smiled, "Hottie 1 and Hottie 2?" I ask confused.

"Okay well there are 2 groups and they both have really hot boys in them, and well we don't know what their name should be but 'Hottie' so yeah" Leanne answered.

"Oh okay now it makes sense" I sarcastically say which made them laugh, "Yeah" Leanne spoke still laughing.

As the bell went we all went to our classes and would meet at break time at the same place, so I headed of to my next lesson which was Music.

As Music finished it was break time so I headed to their usual hang out place and as I arrived there were more people, "Lilac!" Louise embraced me with a tight hug, "C-can't b-breathe" I stutter, "Oh sorry" she giggled.

"Okay so this here is Michelle, then it's Caleb, then Luke, then Rochelle and last Lillian" Louise introduced me to the rest of their group, "Nice to meet you all" I smiled, "BRITISH!" Caleb shouted smiling widely at me, "Yes I am no need to shout for the whole world to hear you" I laughed, "Sorry it's just well their isn't a lot of people with different accents here,

well other than a few but that's it and you're our first British"
his said, "should I be proud?" I ask, "Yes. Yes you should" he
replied looking and sounding serious but still chuckled.

"Lilac, nice name" Rochelle smiled, "I like you're name too" I
smiled, "Hey you're not American?" I ask, "Nah I'm Australian"
she smiled, "Nice I love you're accents!" I randomly say which
made her smile, "Thanks, and I love yours too" she smiled,
"I have a feeling we will be good friends" Rochelle added
making me laugh, "Agreed" I said giggling.

"So Rochelle have you lived here a while?" I ask, "No we
moved here 3 years ago" she answered, "We?" I ask, "Me and
my brother and my parents" she answered, "Oh, nice to know"
I smiled.

"What about you? I mean I know you only got here, but
who with?" she asked, "Me, my little sister who is 10, my 2
older brothers who are 17 and 18 and my parents" I smile,
"My brother is also 17" she said smiling, "Nice" I laugh.

"So why did you move here?" she asked, "Oh, well things
were going on, we wanted to get away and we decied America
so we are here now" I answered a bit quickly because I didn't
want to go into detail, "You?" I ask, "The same thing kind of"
she smiled, "Like I said we would be good friends" she said
laughing again, "Yes! I agree" I say laughing as well.

"Hey what do you have next?" Rochelle asks, "Um, Art I
think" I answer, "Me to!" she yelled happily, "Okay well let's

go the bell just went" I said and we both started to walk to class.

Chapter 4

As we entered the room everyone started at me again, "When will they stop staring?" I asked Rochelle, "God knows" she laughed, "Sit with me at the back" Rochelle said pulling me to the seat next to me. "Okay class we have a new student, Lilac. Lilac in art we have just been doing pieces that describe us so you don't have to worry about anything and Rochelle will help you out" the teacher said so me and Rochelle got up and got our stuff to paint.

"What are you drawing?" I ask, "I'm going to draw a wolf" she replied, "Why?" I ask, "Because a wolf, is something that describes me, it is a mistaken creature with secrets, it is like having 2 personalities, one hidden and the other to be shown. Not having people know what we really feel because they don't understand and also because it's my favourite animal" she laughed, "Wow, I might also have to draw a wolf" I laugh.

"No don't worry I won't I will just draw what I draw I guess" I smile and look at my paper.

I started to draw at first, and I was drawing woods, that got deeper and deeper.

As I painted it I made the colours dark, and misty, I made it look like it was night and scary. As I finished I dried it that added some pencils to make more effect and I was finally done.

"Is this okay?" I asked Rochelle and when her eyes laid on my work her eyes widened.

"Wow, that is amazing! Where did you learn to paint like this?" she asked, "I don't know I just always practiced" I answer.

"So what does this picture mean about you?" she asked.

"Well my life is like a dark gloomy scary forest, it's somewhere where some people wouldnt go. It's depressing, different and contains a secret that only can be found out if you keep going through the woods, but it never ends. It's just my way of saying that I am different that what people expect me to be" I answer, "Wow we have so much in common!" Rochelle said while laughing a bit.

I laughed a bit more and went to hand in my work to the teacher, her eyes also widened, "WOW!" she gasps.

"Oh my- Wow, where did you learn to do this?" she asked, "I don't know, I just practiced a lot I guess" I answered feeling a bit uncomfortable.

"Wow, okay well I'm going to put this on display" she smiled proudly, "Okay" I replied then went to my seat, "I guess she liked it then?" she asked.

"Clearly, she said she will put it on display" I laughed, "Wow" she laughed as well.

As lunch time started me and Rochelle both walked up to out hang out spot.

"Lilac" someone called from behind me and it turns out it was Luca, "Hey Luca what's up?" I ask, "Nothing just came to make sure you okay and nothing bad has happened?" he said trying to make me fess up if anything bad has happened.

"No, I'm fine, I've made friends, and I'm doing well what about you?" I ask, "I'm good, yeah and so is Riley, oh and if anything does happen tell me okay?" he said, "Okay okay I will dad" I said sarcastically, "Good" he replied walking over to his friends.

"Now who. The hell. Was that?" Rochelle asked, "My brother, Luca?" I said, "Why?" I ask, "He is fricken hot!" she smiled, "Okay" I said slowly.

"Sorry, but he really is. You need to introduce me to him but first does he have a girlfriend?" she asks, "Okay you will meet him soon, and no he doesn't" I answered rolling my eyes, "Are both you're brothers hot?" she asked.

"Uh. well I don't think I should be answering that, but they are quite good looking" I say nodding my head, "Okay I want to meet you're family, can I come over today? Pweeeez" she begged, "Okay okay yes you can" I laugh.

"So what about me though, when can I meet you're brother and parents? I ask, "Well I don't know but my brother you can meet whenever he goes to this school, and he is in the "Hottie 1' group" she answered laughing.

"Ha! Well I guess I will meet him soon" I say winking, "Yeah you will don't worry" she laughed at me which I then also laughed along wither her.

"Hey girls!" Leanne said as she approached us, "Hey" we both said, "I see you two have became quick friends" she smiled, "yeah we have" Rochelle smile nudging me.

"Okay well I got to tell you guys something, Nick is throwing a party Friday night, so you two want to join?" Leanne asked with hope in her eyes, I wasn't really sure, but then again I suppose I could.

"Okay but I need to stay round someone's house, I don't want my parents knowing I snuck out" I say, "Stay round mine! Plus my parents are out the weekend for their anniversary" Rochelle said, "Okay I will stay round Rochelle's and we will meet you guys there?" I suggested.

"Nope, we will all stay round Rochelle's" Leanne, smirked, "Yeah, whenever Nick throws parties we all stick together after and stay round someone's house and this time it's Rochelle's so me you Louise, and I think all of the other girls are staying round her house" Leanne said but still asking Rochelle to make sure, "Sure yeah don't worry you can all come round, only Blake will be there I think, maybe a few of his friends" Rochelle said eyeing Leanne when she said 'friends', and that made Leanne's face lit up, "Will Cole be there?" she asked, "Maybe, but I don't know yet we will find out when they are all there" Rochelle answered which made Leanne nod.

As the day ended me and Rochelle both walked to where my mum should be to pick us all up.

I saw my brothers walk up to us and Luca had a smile on his face, "Hey" I said waving.

"Hey" they both said, "Are you going to introduce us to you're pretty friend?" Luca smirked making Rochelle blush, "Rochelle this is Luca, and this is Riley, Riley and Luca this is Rochelle, there you go" I smirk while staring between Rochelle and Luca who were both staring at each other smiling.

I smiled at Riley, while we secretly make fun of Rochelle and Luca, finally mum was here, "Hey mum" I said, "This is my friend Rochelle can she come home with us for a bit today?" I ask and Luca's face immediately lit up.

"Sure honey, Rochelle would you like to stay over for dinner?" mum asked, "Um yes please if you don't mind that is" Rochelle answered politely, "Of course honey, I don't mind at all" my mum replied smiling as we got in.

"Mum where is Willow?" I ask, "She is already home, her school finished before yours" mum answered, "Willow?" Rochelle asked, "My little sister" I answered, "Our little sister" Luca cut in "Fine, 'OUR' little sister" I laughed and so did Rochelle.

As we arrived home me and Rochelle jumped our of the car and ran up to my house, "Wow you're house is nice" she complimented, "Thanks" I reply.

We walk in and I was interrupted by Willow jumping up to hugging me, "Hey Willow" I said hugging her tightly, "Hey!" she replied then I put her down, "Willow this is Rochelle, Rochelle this is Willow" I introduced them.

"Hi" Rochelle said first, Willow was about to laugh, "You like Luca, a lot" she said and started to laugh, Rochelle was blushing like mad, "How did you know that?" she asked.

I just giggled a bit, then talked to Willow through our minds, "Willow stop it you're embarrassing her, and you don't want her finding anything out".

Willow nodded, "Sorry about that" Willow said to Rochelle, "It's okay, don't worry about it but seriously how did you know?" Rochelle asked.

"Well first by the way you looked at him when he walked past you, and then how he started back at you, so there was a connection" she replied, "Wow how old are you?" Rochelle asked, "Ten" Willow replied, "Once again. Wow" Rochelle said looking amazed.

"Okay let's go to my room then" I said and walked heading to my room with Rochelle and Willow following me.

As I got to my room I watched Rochelle's expression, and she looked stunned.

''Wow! You're room is amazing! Did you draw these?'' Rochelle asked heading over to a plain wall with a little bit of my art of it, ''Yeah'' I answered.

''Nice idea right there. Nice. Idea.'' she nodded in approval.

''Overall you're room is amazing!'' she laughed, ''Thanks'' I reply, ''Rochelle, we need to make plans about Friday night'' I say, ''Okay but even with Willow, no affence'' she said a bit quickly.

''Don't worry I don't tell mum anything unless you want me to'' Willow replied, ''Yeah don't worry we are bff's we always keep secrets'' I say smiling ay Willow who was also smiling back.

''Okay then, well tell you're mum you're staying at mine for the night, which you are anyway, then we get ready at mine, leave, party come back, talk and eventually sleep, sound good?'' Rochelle asks, ''Yes, yes it does'' Willow said first trying not to laugh, ''Yeah it does Rochelle, I guess you do this often?'' I ask, ''Yeah sometimes plus I'm always organized so'' Rochelle stated.

''I'm annoyed that I can't come'' Willow said sounding annoyed, ''Me too, but you are sadly to young plus we all know how you are when you're drunk'' I say winking, ''Wait she's been drunk before?'' Rochelle asked clearly amused, ''Yeah, blame Lilac for that! And I hate being ten'' she frowned, ''When we are all of age we will all go out clubbing okay?'' I say, ''Yupp!'' Willow smiled popping the 'P'.

"Girls dinner!" Mum called from downstairs, "Leggo!" I say and walk downstairs, "Hey girls" mum said smiling, "Hey" we all said.

We all sat down and started to eat, "So Lilac how was you're day?" dad asked eyeing me, "Good, I made a few friends" I said, "A few? Lilac I heard you are in the popular group?" Riley smirked, "Maybe, and well they are quite and really nice so okay I made a lot of friends" I smiled, "Good to hear that" dad smiled.

"Oh mum and dad, can I stay round Rochelle's for the night on Friday? There are going to be a few of us it is sort of thing they do every once in a while right Rochelle?" I asked Rochelle, "Yeah we would have sleepovers to catch up and have fun" Rochelle smiles while still eating, "So an I go please?" I ask giving my puppy dog face, "Of course you can" mum said, "Yes you can" Dad also said, "YAY!" I replied high fiving Rochelle.

After dinner Rochelle had to go home so we exchanged phone numbers and hugged each other then she left.

"So Luca, you like Rochelle then huh?" I asked smirking, "What? Psht no" he lamely said, "Yes you do I can sense it!" Willow laughed butting in, "Hey stay out of my head" he moaned, "No can do big bro just handle it" she smirked while laughing.

"Okay I'm going to take a shower then go to bed so you two may continue fighting, but Luca come on we all know you like her" I said winking at Luca before leaving to go to my room.

As I walked in my room I got a towel then headed straight for the shower and washed my hair and myself then slowly got out, dried myself and put my pajamas on then went to bet as I am absolutely tired.

Let's just say this once my face hit that pillow I was out.

Chapter 5

Next day:

My alarm went of again and it is Friday, I groan and went to take a shower to quickly wash myself but not my hair.

I got out and dried myself then went to my walk in wardrobe and decided to wear dark blue skinny jeans and a red tank top with my black jacket and blue converse, I did my usual makeup and brushed my hair a bit, and went downstairs for breakfast.

"Morning!" I say louder this time so everyone noticed me, "Morning" they said in sync, I say down and ate some cereal and a cup of tea again and went to brush my teeth.

"Luca ready?" I ask waiting for him to come downstairs as he is driving us to school in his new car he got.

"Okay I'm here let's go" He smiled so me Luca and Riley got in the car a drove to school.

As we arrived I got out and saw Rochelle smiling at me then at Luca, "Hey" she said to him "Hey beautiful" he winked and walked past us, I could see she was blushing, "I see the wedding bells already" I joked causing her to give me the evils.

We walked over to meet everyone else, "Hey" I said, "Hey" that replied back, "So can you stay round Rochelle's?" Leanne asked, "Yupp!" I smile widely while we all jump excited.

"Oh, but by the way I don't have anything to wear there though" I frown, "You can borrow one of my dresses" Rochelle suggested, "Sure, oh and I will bring tights, I don't really like wearing party dresses without tights is that okay?" I ask, "Go for it" Leanne and Rochelle both say.

As the day went on by it finally came to an end so I got a lift back home with Rochelle to get some clothes, I packed some pajamas, Rochelle insisted on me taking my black bush up bra and matching black underwear, and also some other stuff I need, and my thin black cardigan.

"Luca can you drop me of please?" I call upstairs to Luca, "NO!" he yelled back, "I'm going to Rochelle's" I call back, "Okay I'm coming" he said while speeding down the stairs, "Okay let's go" he said so we all went to his car and went to her house.

"So are you going to that kid Nick's party?" Luca asked, "Uh, w-what?" I stutter, "Don't act stupid, I know you, but don't worry I won't tell. I'm going as well I think so as long as you don't tell I won't" Luca said.

"Deal" I agree, "Okay this is my house" Rochelle said which made Luca stop his car, "See you both tonight then" he winked at Rochelle then hugged me, "Will do, bye!" I say and get out of the car and headed to Rochelle's house.

"You're house looks amazing! I said to Rochelle, "Thanks, oh my brother is here by the way" she said smiling, "Blake isn't it?" I ask, "Yeah" she replied, so with that we walked up to her house and as we entered, Leanne, Louise, Chloe Jade, Michelle and Lillian jumping up to us.

"Finally we've been waiting, okay now let's get ready!" Leanne giggled making us all rush up to I'm guessing Rochelle's room which was amazing and huge.

"Okay well we should get our outfit sorted first okay?" Leanne suggested, "Sure" everyone said, "I'm going to get a drink quickly" I say, "Go for it" Rochelle smiled, so I walked downstairs and went to find the kitchen and when I found it, I started to look for a cup, "Top right cupboard" A deep husky voice from behind me said, I jumped a little startled by his presence.

I turned around and looked at him, I heard him mumble something but he did say it loud enough for me to hear, but I let it go.

Now let me say he is fricken sexy, he has dirty blond hair with bright blue eyes, a few freckles and well built.

He was toned but not too toned, just perfect I guess, I smiled, and opened the cupboard where he said where the cups were and sure enough there was, "Thanks" I mumble and walked over to the tap getting some water.

"No problem" He smiled, "I'm Blake by the way" he introduced, "Oh you're Rochelle's brother, well nice to meet you, I'm Lilac" I introduced back.

"Nice to meet you" he winked, "So you're going to that Nick's party?" he asked, "Yeah, what about you?" I asked taking a sip of my drink, "Yeah me and my friends are going then we will come back here." he answered, "So I guess I will see you there and back here" I smiled, "I will make sure of it" he smiled back.

I finished my drink and placed it in the sink, "I better go before they hunt me down to try on all the clothes" I giggled, "Okay, well I will see you later then" he smiled while I walked upstairs to Rochelle's room.

"Found me anything yet?" I asked, "YES!" Leanne, Rochelle and Louise shouted holding up a darkish red colour dress that stops at mid thigh and had long sleeves with a diamond cut out where my hips would be.

It was perfect, "YES!" I agree with them, "Thought you would like it" Rochelle smiled, "I love it, oh and I met Blake by the way" I smiled slightly blushing at the thought of him, "What did he say?" Rochelle asks, "He said he is coming to Nick's party, and some of his friends will stay round after" I reply, "Okay" Rochelle replied smiling.

After a few hours we were all ready, my hair was in it's natural curliness style but in a high ponytail, and I wore my dress with black tights and red heels.

My makeup had a smokey affect and some liquid eye liner and some lip gloss.

I was now finished to I waited for everyone else who were nearly done, then there was a knock at the door, I answered it and saw Blake smiling at me while checking me out, "Just wondering do you want me to give you lifts there and back, I'm not drinking tonight" he suggested, "Um sure I guess so" I smile looking into his eyes and they were locked for a few seconds until Rochelle came to the door, "Okay you can go now we will be downstairs in a minute' Rochelle said closing the door staring at me with a smirk, "You know he likes you right?" she asked, "What?" I ask confused, "He really likes you" she winked then walked away, okay then.

Once we were all done we left downstairs to see Blake with five other guys but my eyes never left Blakes as our eyes lock again, my heart beating a lot faster than usual, and I'm sure who ever is next to me can here it but oh well.

As we walked downstairs we all got into Blakes car and left for the party.

Chapter 6

"Hey" Blake said while smiling at me, "Hello" I replied smiling back, "You look gorgous" he smirked, "Thanks, you look good to" I giggled but still blushed.

"Come on let's go Blake!" Rochelle demanded, "Okay okay I'm coming" Blake replied rolling his eyes getting in his car, but after he let me in, what a gentlemen.

As we arrived at the party it was huge already, I walked in with Rochelle and Louise by my side and Blake behind us walking over to his group of friends that I'm guessing are part of the 'Hottie 1' group.

"Want a drink?" Louise asked, "No thanks, I am not the best under the influence of alcohol" I laugh, "Okay then but if you want one just grab one okay" Louise said laughing with me.

I walked up to Rochelle who was actually with my brother, "Hey Luca" I smirk, "Hey Rochelle" I smirk again, "Hey" they both said in sync not looking at me but each other, God their cuteness is killing me.

"Lilac you're drinking are you?" Luca suddenly asks suspiciously, "No I'm not you know what I'm like when I'm drunk"

I wink smiling, "Oh yeah, true so no drinks for you then" he winked back which I nodded to.

I walk away to get some fresh air, and we have been here for a couple hours now so I'm am wondering when we will go home, "H-heyey th-there!" Nick said walking (more like sliding) over to me clearly very drunk.

"Hey" I smile trying not to laugh as he looked at his hands looking confused about something, "I w-was told I'm drunk but I've only had like" he stopped while trying to count on his fingers, "More than 50 but that isn't a lot so I'm very confused" he slurred while sitting next to me.

"Hate to say it but Nick you are very. Very. Very drunk, go home okay you don't want to drink anymore" I smile while rubbing his back.

"But I-I don't want to go home I am perfectly fine here" he whined crossing his arms, "Okay but don't drink anymore okay you don't want to get anymore drunk than you already are" I laugh while patting his back.

"Okay okay, hey why aren't you drinking?" he asked, "I don't drink" I reply looking at my hands, "Please one drink for me?" he begged, "No!" I warn making him look upset.

"I got to go now" I smile getting up walking away but he grabbed me by my waist, "Give me a kiss first" he demanded, "No, get off me!" I begged annoyed, "No come one kiss" he demanded again but I just kept trying to push him of.

Out of nowhere he pressed his lips on mine forcefully as I struggled to escape his arms.

I was moving my head around trying to avoid his face but he pressed me up against the wall once again pressing his lips against mine.

I could smell the alcohol which made me want to be sick.

I kept trying to push him of but he wouldn't budge but out of nowhere he was pushed of me by someone and was now on the ground with someone on him.

It took me a while to realize who it was, and it turns out it was Blake, "DON'T YOU EVER TOUCH HER AGAIN!" he shouted right in his face.

He got up and walked up to me, "Are you okay?" he asked with a worried tone, "I'm fine, thankyou" I smile about to walk away but he pulled me into a tight but welcoming hug.

"Good" he whispered in my ear sending shivers all over my body, as he let me go we walked back inside the house and went to get the girls, "Rochelle come on let's go now" I said while pulling her arm.

She pouted at me because she was with Luca, "You two can kiss each other more tomorrow right now we need to get home" I laugh as I pulled her up and away, "Bye Luca" I called out which he waved back in return, "Where is everyone else?" I ask.

As we got everyone including Blakes friends we all returned to Rochelle's house.

Chapter 7

"What can we do now?" Leanne asked a little bit drunk, "Um we can play truth or dare?" Cole suggested while staring at Leanne smiling which made Leanne blush.

"OKAY!" Rochelle shouted while she ran to the living room which we all followed and sat in a big circle.

"Oh but first boys I think you need to introduce yourself" Rochelle said looking at Blake and his friends.

"Okay well I will go first. I'm Cole and 17, and have been friends with Blake since we were 10" Cole said smiling, he was quite good looking, he had black hair with bright blue eyes and quite tanned.

"Well let me just say, we are all 17 years old okay, and I'm Elliot" he smiled, Elliot has bright blonde hair and golden brown eyes and also tanned.

"I'm Noah!" Noah shouted waving his hand like a crazy person, which made me laugh, Noah has light brown hair and green eyes and also tanned, so basically they are all tanned.

"And I'm Leon" Leon said smiling with a wink, Leon has dark brown hair with some highlights and green-blue eyes.

"Okay now we are all introduced let's play!" Rochelle spoke loudly clearly excited, "Okay I will start" Rochelle smiled evilly.

"Cole, truth or dare?" Rochelle smirked, "Dare" he replied acting all tough.

"Kiss Leanne" Rochelle grinned, so Cole got up and walked over to Leanne and gave her a full on kiss, which was cute but also disturbing.

"My turn!" Cole said, "Okay um, Lila, truth or dare?" Cole asked me, "Um, truth, I'm a whimp" I smile.

"Okay um what is you're biggest secret?" Cole asked making everyone look at me, "Um I have quite a few so I will tell you one which is the reason why I moved here" I started which everyone nodded to.

"Well at my school I was bullied a lot, physically and verbally. I don't know what I did to make them bully me but I never asked, them. Anyway well I never told my parents but one time it got to out of hand so I tried to kill myself, but my brother found me in the act and took me to the hospital, so once I got out I had to tell my parents what has been happening. They got me a therapist which was no help so they decided a fresh new start would help and America was their thought" I admit looking down at my hands.

"W-why would anyone bully you?" Blake asked looking like he would cry, "I don't know" I whispered, "Aw, don't worry Lilac you have us now!" Leanne smiled which everyone nodded to answer.

"Okay Lilac you're turn" Rochelle encouraged trying to lighten up the mood, "Okay um, Rochelle truth or dare?" I ask smirking hoping she would pick truth.

"Truth" she shyly answered, "What feelings do you have for my brother?" I asked giving her the eye mockingly.

"Uh, I um he is um well I guess I really like him" she answered blushing like mad, "Good to know" I smirked.

So basically the game continued for ages until we got bored. "Okay what now?" I ask, "Um well, OH YEAH I HAVE AN IDEA!" Rochelle screamed, "Okay tell us but don't shout please" I say laughing while rubbing my ears.

"Okay we can play hide n seek in the dark!" she suggested which everyone cheered to.

Rochelle decided to be the seeker so we all hid, I went to the first place I would always hide which was in the garden.

I ran outside walking near some bushes to hide behind, I sat on the grass and played with the grass.

I heard some footsteps so I tried to make myself as quiet as possible, but then I realised that it was Blake.

"Jesus I thought I was caught!" I sighed of relief, "Sorry I just followed you out here" he smirked.

"Why?" I ask, "Because I wanted to make sure you were okay, you know about everything" he said comforting me, "Yeah I'm fine now, I mean yeah it is still hard but I'm getting better." I answered while leaning my head on his shoulder.

"Are you sure, like did you do anything to yourself? That you shouldn't of done?" he asked trying to hint me to confessing, "Well yeah I tried to commit suicide" I scoffed, "How did you try to commit suicide?" he asked, "I slit my wrists a multiple of times, and my stomach" I replied looking and feeling ashamed, but to my surprise he pulled me into another hug.

"I won't that anything like that happen to you again!" he promised, I snuggled my head further into his neck, "Thankyou" I whispered.

He raised his head and stared into my eyes making our eyes lock, we stared a little while longer before we started to lean in, and without any hesitation we pushed our lips together kissing passionately and slowly.

The kiss started to get a bit more heated and Blake lifted my up onto his lap so I was straddling him.

I wrapped my arms around his neck while he did the same around my waist.

He pushed my closer in him creating no space between us, I moaned into the kiss which made Blake smile and lick my lower lip asking for entrance which I granted.

We didn't stop making out for what felt like seconds until someone spoke, "Uh, well I was going to say found you put

I will leave you to it" Rochelle winked while walking away giggling to herself.

"That wasn't awkward at all" I laughed, "Nope" Blake replied leaning his forehead on mine as our eyes lock again.

Before I knew it we both started kiss again, and let me tell you something, there were sparks everywhere every time!

We had to stop because someone was shouting, "Love birds you need to come inside now!" Rochelle shouted from the back door.

We both groaned and got up holding each other hands, "Hey there love birds!" Cole laughed, "Shut up!" Blake warned, "Okay okay calm down!" Cole laughed again.

We all went into the living room again and decided to watch films, "Hey what time is it?" I ask, "Um half two in the morning I think" Louise replied, "Oh my God haha" I said while laughing.

We decided to watch Scary Movie 3 as well it's funny and awesome!

I was sitting next to Blake and Rochelle, but half way through the film I felt a bit tired so I leaned my head on Blake's shoulder slowly falling asleep.

Next Day:

I woke up the next day in someones arms, as I looked around I noticed I was still in the living room and it was Blake that wrapped his hands around my waist.

I smiled and cuddled into his chest listening to his smooth heart beat.

"Morning princess" he had which made me jump, he chuckled at me then opened his eyes, "Morning" I greeted back, "Nice sleep?" he asks, "Yeah what about you?" I ask back, "Good" he replied smiling at me and stroking my hair.

I snuggled back into his chest listening to his hear beat again, "Where is everyone?" I ask, "The girls went into Rochelle's room, and the boys went home" he answered while still playing with my hair, "Not to be rude, but why are we like this? Like why are we so intimate, because we have known each other for like 2 days or something?" I ask, I know it wasn't kind but I was just confused at how close I am to him already.

"Well there are some things you will find out which partly answers your question, but for now I guess you could say your instincts trust me" he answered clearly trying to make it sound less confusing than it is, but it didn't work that well.

"Oh" I replied still confused but I didn't push the subject further.

"Do you want some breakfast?" he asks, "Um okay" I say back smiling.

He gets up taking his arms away from my waist making me pout wanting his warmth back but I quickly stopped as I realized what I was doing, but he noticed my pouting and chuckled at me making me blush slightly.

We head to the kitchen and start to make pancakes, "We going to make some for everyone?" I ask, "Yupp!" Blake replies popping the 'P'.

I walk upstairs to Rochelle's room to tell everyone to come down as the pancakes were nearly done, I walked into Rochelle's room to see everyone asleep, "Girls, pancakes, nearly done, wake up now" I say slowly but loudly so they can hear me hopefully and luckily they did as their heads shot straight up, "Pancakes?" Louise mumbled slowly waking up fully.

"Yes, now come downstairs if you want so-" I was cut of as they all ran past me sprinting downstairs leaving me amazed.

I walk downstairs to see everyone tucking into their pancakes already, wow, I walked up to the empty seat which was next to Blake and Leanne.

I sat down and start to tuck in and in the end I ate the total of 3 pancakes whereas everyone else had like 5 which amazed me again.

"You lot are all pigs" I exclaim while grinning widely. "No we just have a large appetite" Leanne replied defending herself and the others, "Suuuurreee" I dragged which made them all roll their eyes.

As I finished I put my plate in the sink and washed it, "What are we doing today then?" I ask turning around looking at everyone, well when I say everyone I mean Blake, what? You can not judge me.

Blake gasped, "What?!" I ask worried, "Your eyes, they changed colour?" I said in more of a question, his expression was like her was confused but then he smiled, "That is amazing!" he smiled, "What colour were they?" I ask, "purpley blue" he answered observing my eyes.

"Awesome, that colour is different!" I exclaim, "What do they change colour all the time?" Leanne asks, "Yeah, so far they have turned grey, bright blue and grass green" I answer while looking at everyone's amazed facial expression, "Wow!" they all said in sync.

I smile and laugh a bit, "So back to the question what can we do today?" I ask, "Well I was thinking can we all go to you're house?" Rochelle suggested, "Uh, I guess so" I smile, "Yay, you guys will meet her awesome little sister!" Rochelle giggled, "Yeah, oh shit, uh can you all come over later I need to do something with Willow for a bit?" I ask while standing up, "Yeah sure we need to get more clothes anyway" Leanne answered while the rest nod, "Okay well I will see you in a bit" I say starting to walk towards the front door.

"Hey wait, want me to drive you home?" Blake asks, "Sure!" I answer smile while I open to door heading to Blake's car.

We walk inside the car and start to drive to my house, "So what are you and Willow doing then?" Blake asks, "Uh well I can't tell you but maybe in the future I can" I answer while looking at my hands.

"Okay, oh but what ever you do don't go into those woods" Blake said out of no where.

"Why?" I ask, "Well there are some things in there that you don't want to see or be near" he answered while looking intensely at the road.

"What ever they are, I am pretty sure I can handle myself" I said.

"No you can't, I'm sorry but please just don't go in there, at least not today" he said as he parked outside of my house, "Fine" I answer while getting out of the car waving bye to him.

I walked inside my house to be greeted by Willow, "Are we going to the woods again?" she asked with hope in her eyes.

"Yes of course we are!" I smirk, okay I'm sorry but no one will stop us practising and the woods is the only place we can do it without being caught.

Chapter 8

We both get ready, I was wearing light blue ripped shorts with a black lace top and black slip on shoes.

I walk downstairs to meet Willow, "Let's go!" I say, "Bye mum!" we both shout and leave the house heading towards the woods.

As we enter the forest we both head to the same spot we went to before.

"Lilac, I have a bad feeling about this" Willow states, "Don't worry it will be fine" I try to confirm which works.

"What should we do then?" Willow asks, "Call upon nature?" I suggest which Willow eagerly nodded to.

We linked hands again, we had linked together, and now we want nature to respond.

Moments later the leaves and trees were responding by moving around us, but we had to stop as we heard a noise.

"What was that?" Willow asks, "Try to see it" I said, she nodded and looked around then back at me.

"Wolf?" she said confused, "A big wolf, there is quite a few, they are heading out way" she said then realized what she said.

We started to run away but I was pinned down by a big light brown wold, it was growling at me.

"Willow run home, don't tell mum, I will be fine!" I mind linked to Willow.

"But Lilac, I can-" I cut her of, "LEAVE!" I yell through mind link which she responded by running away.

The wolf growled at me, I was scared but I didn't show it to the wolf, which made it grow again.

Suddenly the wolf was tackled of me by another bigger black wolf, I was confused but I kept watching, they were full on attacking each other.

I felt bad for the black wolf as it saved me, I used my magic to create wind, I moved my hand in the direction I wanted to wind to pull the light brown wolf into.

And just like that the wolf was thrown at a tree where as the black one passed out, I ran up to it to see if it was okay.

Out of no where it turned into a human, I gasped as I realized who it was.

Blake.

Chapter 9

I sat there for a couple of minutes waiting for him to wake up, then he started to move around, he woke up then saw me, his eyes widened.

"Lilac, I uh why did you come to the woods?!" he demanded, "What are you?!" I also demanded, then I realized he was naked, "Um, where are you're clothes?" I ask, "Shredded" he replied.

I groaned then made clothes appear, "Put them on!" I said while throwing them at him, "I'm done" he said so I turned around.

"Now why are you a werewolf?" I ask, "I was born one, so was Rochelle, that really is it, but what about you? How did you make him move and then make clothes appear?" he asked clearly confused.

"I'm a witch, so is my sister Willow, we were practising when that wolf appeared, you tackled him of me, I some reason felt worried about you so I got him of you making him hit a tree, but you past out, and I have been waiting for you to wake up" I answer while looking deep into his eyes.

"Oh yeah, now can you tell me why I feel this way about you?" I ask, "Well you are um" he started, "You're my mate, I didn't understand how you could feel the connection since you're not a wolf, but I guess because you're supernatural that might be how" he answered.

"Mate?" I whispered, "Yeah a mate is a werewolves true love, where they are made for each other, their soul mates they other half to the werewolf" he said looking slightly embarrassed, "What, so I'm you're soul mate?" I ask hopefully it was a yes.

"Yes" he answered looking into my eyes with a hint of hope, "Finally!" I smile with tears in my eyes as I run into Blake's arms, "Huh?" Blake asked as he snuggled into my neck, "I finally have someone I know I am meant to be with" I answer

"I'm glad to be that person" he whispered in my ears sending goosebumps down my spine.

We stayed like that for a while until I realized something.

"SHIT!" I exclaimed, "What?!" Blake asked sounding worried, "Willow, she left I need to make sure she is okay!" I start.

"Willow, hey are you okay?" I ask through mind link.

"Oh my God, are you okay, yeah I'm fine I told mum that you were at a friends, but are you okay?" Willow asks back.

"I'm fine Blake saved me, he is a werewolf okay, he saved me though, and he knows I'm a witch" I sigh.

"WHAT?! Wow I thought I felt something different when I was there, and will he keep our secret?" Willow said.

"Yeah he will, okay he looks confused now so see you when I'm home bye!" I end and look back at Blake.

"I was mind linking Willow so she knows I'm okay" I answer knowing he is thinking what was I doing.

"Mind link? Wow werewolves can do that as well" he replied excitedly, I just rolled my eyes.

"I think she should go back now" I said and start walking, "Okay" Blake answered walking along side me and slowly taking my hand in his hand.

"So what do else do I need to know about you?" Blake asks, "What do you mean?" I ask back, "What else is there I should know about you or your magic?"

"Well, um our family has been witches for 500 years, some of our family possesses the power of shape shifting, or things to do with the elements, I on the other hand well I don't know what I am exactly because my grand mother told me I had something else in my blood that others don't have, I don't know what it is, but I know I'm a witch, I have the power to control all elements, I don't know the rest but apparently when I find the other half of me that's when I find them" I answered, "Wow" Blake replied in complete shock.

As we arrive ay my house I am attacked with a huge hug from Willow, "Thank god you're okay" she whispered, "Shh, it's okay, I'm fine" I say calmly.

"Wait a second, that's the wolf?" She said, I nodded, "I can smell him?" she giggled, "Yeah so can I" I giggle along with her, "What are you to giggling at?" he asked, "We can smell you" Willow answered which he answered by giving us a weird look, "We can sense stuff, and well there is sometimes a smell, and I can smell you, but to be honest I smelt you on the first day at school I just didn't realize." I say while blushing.

"What? How? Only wolves and vampires can smell other wolves and vampires?" Blake asked, mine and Willows head shot straight up.

"What is that supposed to mean then?" I ask, "I don't know" Blake replied, "Lilac, we need to contact her" Willow said, I knew who she meant.

"I know, come on let's do it in my room" I say back and head to my room with both Willow and Blake behind me.

We walk into my room and I quickly closed my door, "Willow block out the sound so know one can hear us" I order Willow which she nods to and does the spell.

"Done" Willow told me, "Okay Blake sit down on the bed and don't say anything" I order again, Blake did as I said, so now me and Willow linked hands, "Grandma" we called.

A shimmery light appeared and then Grandma appeared, "Willow? Lilac? What am I doing here?" she asked, "Grandma, what are we? Please answer me now" I snap, I know it was rude but she needs to tell me now.

Chapter 10

''**I** see you found you're mate, as I found mine'' Grandma smiled looking at Blake who looked quite confused, ''Yeah, but what am I? Am I a wolf or something, how do I have a mate? And how can I smell him?'' I ask getting annoyed she won't answer me.

''I am a quarter wolf, and you're mum is full wolf, it runs through you're blood. You are part witch and part wolf'' my Grandma finally answers.

''Well that explains a lot'' Blake says chuckling.

''Yeah, I know sorry I never told you before though Lilac, I needed you to find you're mate before, but then I died, I knew you would call for me though'' Grandma smiled at me.

''Why did I have to wait until I found my mate?'' I ask.

''Once you meet you're mate that is when you turn into a wolf, you couldn't turn before because you're not a full wolf until you find you're other half which would be you're mate'' Grandma states.

''You're saying, I'm going to turn into a wolf? When?!'' I ask while freaking out.

"Well you met you're mate today so, the next full moon which is tonight, because it's on the full moon is because of you're witch side, they connect, once you changed once you can control when you want to change" Grandma told me while smiling.

"Yay" I reply with a sarcastic tone, "I will be there with you!" Blake confirmed while he gripped hold of my waist.

"Good" I whispered while I put my head on his neck breathing in his scent.

"Okay well I'm going to go now, nice seeing you both, nice meeting you" my Grandma said awkwardly, "Bye nanna" Willow replied, "Bye nanna" I also reply.

And with that she disappeared.

"Wow, that isn't something you see everyday" Blake laughed slightly, "In our world it is" Willow laughed back.

"Yeah so you're both witches then?" he asked, "Yeah I am also a witch, when Lilac found out she told me and well she told me that she could feel energy of me giving me a clue that I was also one, then we talked to nanna about it and she told us everything- Well almost everything" Willow answered for him sighing.

"Does it hurt when you turn for the first time?" I ask feeling scared, "A bit, but I will comfort you okay? I promise" Blake spoke while kissing my cheek.

"Uh dudes, you're friends are at the door in 3, 2,-" Ding Dong "1" Willow smirked.

We all laughed and walked downstairs to greet everyone inside. I opened the door and saw only Rochelle, Leanne and Louise, "Where are the others?" I ask, "They had to go home, hey Blake" Rochelle answered while winking at Blake.

"Come on in" I said and let them in, "Oh by the way I noticed you had a swimming pool so I told the girls and we brought our bathing suits hope you don't mind" Rochelle told me, "I don't mind" I answered back smiling, "Hey what about me?" Blake asked, "I brought yours as well" Rochelle said rolling her eyes.

Us girls went in my room to put on our bath suits, I am wearing a black bikini with white stripes.

"Ready?" I ask which everyone eagerly nodded to so we all walked downstairs and saw both Luca and Riley.

"Hey girls" Luca smirked while clearly checking Rochelle out, "Hey, you all going swimming?" Riley asked, "Yeah we are, Blake is already out there I think" I answered, "Blake?" Riley asked while wriggling his eyebrows.

"You will meet him in a second okay" I laugh and start heading downstairs.

We all walked downstairs and then I saw Blake waiting for us in the kitchen as he saw me I knew he checked me out which made me blush.

He walked up to me then gave me a hug, "I missed you" he whispered into my neck, which made me shiver, "Missed you to" I whisper back.

As we broke away from our hug I realized everyone left for the pool, "Okay then" I laugh.

We both walked outside hand in hand, "Ready?" Blake asked, "Ready for wh-" I was cut of as he ran pulling me with him and we jumped into the pool.

"Oh ready for that" I giggled, "Yeah" he laughed back.

We kept swimming and splashing each other while everyone else did the same, "Lilac!" Willow screamed, I looked up and saw the fear she had, "What?" I ask getting out of the pool grabbing my towel, "The full moon, starts in half an hour" she tells me, "Oh my God I completely forgot!" I said while freaking out.

Blake came out from the pool and hugged me from behind, "What's up?" he asked clearly worried, "The full moon starts in half an hour, I need to go now" I whispered then ran into my room.

I got changed into leggings and a plain black top with a jacket and vans.

I walk back down stairs, "Lilac, I'm coming with you!" Blake states, "Okay where can I go?" I ask, "'The woods" he replies so without another word we both start to run to the woods.

We finally arrived at the woods, "When will the full moon start?" I ask, "Five minutes" Blake replied looking at me with a worried expression.

We stayed there for a few minutes until an excruciating pain merged.

I couldn't handle this pain, but all I remember was looking at my pure snow white fur before passing out...

Chapter 11

N ext Day

I woke up in a bed, not mine, nor is this my room, I got out of the bed and let me say this, my body feels like sh*t it aches so much.

"Morning sleeping beauty" A deep voice from behind me spoke, I knew who it was, "Hey" I yawned, "What time is it?" I asked, "Um half past one" Blake replied while he handed me some pancakes, "Thank youuuuu" I dragged which caused him to role his eyes.

"So can you tell me what happened?" I asked while shoving pieces of my delicious pancakes.

"Well, I don't know really, first you were transforming, which by the way. You're one good looking wolf" He started while winking making me blush.

"Then?" I asked, "Then you blacked out, and when you did you're fur glowed, or you did, well I don't know but you just glowed and then you were like lifted up from the ground, then you're claws grew longer and sharper, and then you're eyes opened up at first I thought you were awake but then you're eyes changed into a black colour with silver specks here and there, then you looked up to the moon and then. You fell back down to the ground" He told me while I nodded.

"Ohh" I spoke back slowly nodding my head, "Yeah, I waited for a while until you turned back, which you did when the full moon was over" Blake added.

"Oh okay well Blake do you think I could have some painkillers, my head is killing, and my body aches" I complained while giving him puppy dog eyes.

"Okay okay no need to bring the doggies eyes into this" he chuckled while getting me some painkillers.

I giggled at him and sat there while I ate the rest of my pancakes.

By the time I finished Blake came back in with painkillers and a glass of water.

"Thanks" I said as I take the painkillers, "You're welcome" he replied back smiling.

"So what are we going to do today?" Blake asks, "Don't know, but first I should probably tell Willow that I'm okay" I reply, "Okay sure do you want to go now?" Blake asks, "Um, okay" I say back while getting of the bed, "By the way am I at you're house?" I question, "Yupp" he says while popping the 'P'.

"God he is hot" A voice in my head said, "Who said that?" I ask as I look around, "Who said what?" Blake asked, "Never mind" I reply.

"God just kiss him!" The voice appeared again, "Blake, there is a problem!" I said while freaking out.

"What's up?" he asked, "There is a voice in my head" I answer feeling like a fool, "Ha! Saying?" he asked, "Uh, um well, it said you're hot and I should kiss you" I tell him looking at my feet.

"That's you're wolf speaking" Blake explained while laughing, "So my wolf is talking about kissing you? Wow" I spoke shocked.

"We're mates, our bond is really strong especially between our wolfs" he explained again, I grinned, "So you're wolf tells you to kiss me as well then" I said while grinning like a fool.

"All. The. Damn. Time" he replied and every word he said he took a step closer to me until we were so close that I could feel his breath on me, "Good" I said back to while pecking his lips before we continue to get out of his house.

We walk to his car and get in then start to drive home.

"God our mate is sexy" My wolf purred adoring the mate we have, "I know calm down please" I say back to her "I can't calm down, he is right there looking sexy, come on mate with him already!" she demanded, "Mate with him?" I ask, "Basically make love with him, become one!" she told me.

I decided to ignore her now so I pushed her away and looked outside, "Having a conversation with you're wolf?" Blake asked me.

"Yeah, how do you know?" I ask, "My wolf and her are talking" he explained, "Oh" I said back.

"Lilac! What is going on, how are you?" this was Willow, "I'm fine, and I'm on my way back now" I told her, "Okay good, oh and by the way, who was I just talking to? I was trying to talk to you but I was talking to someone else?" Willow asked.

"That would be my wolf" I told her "Oh okay see you in a bit" Willow said then was gone.

We arrive at my house, then I was tackled by Willow, "Are you okay?" she asked with a worried tone, "Willow, I'm fine just a bit achey" I respond which she smiled at.

We walked into my house, "Hey hunny have a nice sleep over at Rochelle's?" mum asked me, "Uh yeah it was cool" I smile then look at Blake who tried to look innocent.

"Good good, well I'm going shopping with you're dad we will most likely be around two hours okay so no parties" mum joked, "Scouts honour" I replied.

She just rolled her eyes and soon left with dad, Blake went in the kitchen so I went to my room to get changed.

As I finished getting changed I left my room and a smell instantly appeared.

It smells like coconut and chocolate, a smile came to my face, but what could possess this smell?

"Mate. Mate. Go to mate!" My wolf cried clearly waning to be with her mate if I wasn't mistaken.

I walked downstairs and entered the kitchen where the smell intensified.

"Um Blake?" I started, "Yeah?" he replied, "What is that smell?" I asked with my eyes closed.

I heard him chuckle, "Um Lilac?" he started making me open my eyes then I realized how close we were, "That smell would be me" he told me which made me blush.

"Huh?" I asked very confused, "Well a werewolf would find their mate through their scent, and whatever their scent is it would be good and the wolf would want more of it, which is kind of how we find our mates" he explained.

I nodded, "What do I smell like?" he asked, "Coconuts and chocolate" I smiled while breathing in his scent.

"What about me?" I ask curious to what my scent is, "Cherries and vanilla perfectly mixed" he replied while staring into my eyes intensely.

He leaned in closer to my face, "Hello!" a voice chirped, it was Rochelle.

"Hey!" I said back smiling at her.

As she walked in she breathed in and then had a confused look on her face.

"Wolf?" was all she said, "Oh, um well I- Uh" I had no idea what to say, thank God Blake was here.

"Okay well we have a lot to tell you, first Lilac is a witch. Turns out she is part wolf. She turned for her first time last night and passed out so I brought her to ours, she woke up this morning and she wanted to come home to tell her sister she is okay" Blake told her, she nodded slowly.

"Oh! And I have found my mate" Blake blurted smiling like a lunatic.

"Who is?" Rochelle asked but was looking at me smirking.

"If it isn't already obvious, my mate is LILAC!" he shouted smiling then pulled me into a tight side hug.

"Aw, but how exactly did she turn for her first time last night?" Rochelle asked, "Well my grandma told me when I summoned her from the dead, she said once I found my mate, the wolf inside me would come out and I would turn on the next fall moon which was that night" I explained.

"Oh, well now I don't know what to say except congrats big bro!" Rochelle states while lightly punching Blake.

"Oh and what are you doing here then? Hmm" I asked while smirking as she blushed, "Well, um, I may of stayed round with Luca, but I swear we didn't do the dirty deed okay we just talked watched films and stuff okay!" Rochelle said in a rush to make sure we understood.

I rolled my eyes, and went to make a drink.

As I got some water I sat down, then Willow came up to me, "Lilac, I saw something" she said with a clear feeling of fear in her eyes.

She started to scare me, "Willow what's wrong? What did you see?" I asked, she looked like she would cry.

"Look" was all she said so she moved her hand to my forehead and was sending me what she saw.

A few minutes later

I gasped really loudly holding my heart, I was crying now, "NO!" I warned, "You're not going to die!" I state pulling her into a tight hug.

"But Lilac, I saw my death, how can we stop it, I don't know when it will happen or why" she sighs while crying on my shoulder.

"We will find out okay" I tell her reassuringly, she nods back at me then gives me a small smile.

Chapter 12

Next Day...

The next day I woke up with Willow laying next to me, she couldn't sleep last night so she stayed in my room.

I got up slowly so I wouldn't wake her up, then left to my bathroom.

I got in the shower and washed my hair and myself, I got out then dried my hair and doing my usual makeup.

I left the bathroom to go to my wardrobe, and decided to wear jean shorts with black patterned tights, and a light blue tank top and a grey cardigan along with plaine black flats.

As I got changed in the bathroom I came back in my room and saw Willow slowly waking up, "hey" I said soothingly, "Hi" she whispered back while yawning.

"Where are you going?" she asked, "I have school silly, do you mind?" I ask.

"No go for it, I will mind link you" she confirmed giving me a light smile.

I walk downstairs and grab an apple, "Luca?!" I call up the stairs, "Just coming!" he called back.

Riley came down first, "Hey" he smiled, "Hello" I chirped back making him role his eyes.

We both waited a couple more minutes then finally Luca walks downstairs.

"It's about time" Riley exclaims, we all laugh a little then leave in Luca's car to school.

We finally arrive at school and as soon as I leave the car, his scent hits me, I smile and look around then see him looking at me smiling, I run up to him and gave him a tight hug.

"Hey to you to" he whispered in my ear sending shivers down my spine.

We stay in each others arms for a while just enjoying the company.

"Are you going to stay like that all day or?" Elliot asked snapping us out of our trance.

I never noticed at first but now I realize that Elliot is a wolf.

"You're a wolf?" I ask, Elliot instantly became confused, "Yeah, and I can see, well smell that you are as well" he winked, "Yeah Lilac Elliot, Cole, Leon and Noah are all wolves including me" Blake informs me.

"Ah okay" I reply nodding my head, "So tell me something Lilac, why can I only now smell you're wolf?" Elliot asks, "I just turned for my first time on Saturday night, I'm a witch and part wolf so once I found my mate I would then turn" I explain.

"Oh well now it makes sense" he chuckled "Yeah" I giggled while leaning into Blake's chest.

At that second I could smell something, it smelt a bit of, not like a wolf but something else, "Blake. What's that smell?" I ask looking into his eyes.

He looks at me worried, "Vampires" was all he said, I looked around and saw the 'Hottie 2' group walking together, well this school is weird isn't it, the 'Hottie 1' group are werewolf's, and the 'Hottie 2' group are vampires, what's next?

"Vampires? Why are they at school then?" I ask, he just shrugged and stared intensely at them.

One of them looked at me and smirked, he had black hair and from what I can see he has blue eyes and a pale face, most likely quite toned as well.

Blake growled at him and stepped in front of me as if to tell him, she-is-mine-so-fuck-off.

I hugged Blake from behind to calm him down which worked as was no longer tense and turned around then hugged me back.

"Don't worry, I won't let him touch you!" he vowed while putting his head in my neck, I think he was sniffing me.

"Thanks, I won't go near him" I replied then kissed his cheek.

"Let's go to class" I tell him, he groans but listens so we both head to our class which we both had together surprisingly, then again I was in the higher set for Science.

As we walked in class all eyes were on us, "Blake?" I asked, "Don't worry babe" he replied.

We walked to our seats, luckily we had a cover teacher so we didn't have to do much work.

So throughout the lesson we were just mucking about.

"Blake why don't you like the vampires?" I asked, he tensed up a bit, "They just are annoying, and well their dead, they think they are all that, and also because Rochelle was, well she was ra-raped by one back in Australia, that is why we moved, so we could start fresh, this happened before she turned so she couldn't fight him of" lake admitted while playing with my hand.

"I'm so sorry. I can't believe someone would do that to anyone" I replied disgusted, Rochelle is like my best friend, correction she is my best friend.

"It isn't you're fault, don't worry, we are all better now, and yeah, but that is why I don't want you near them, I won't let anything like that happen to you ever!" he stated while staring into my eyes.

"Promise?" I say, "Promise" he says firmly.

Chapter 13

A Few Hours Later

It is now lunch time, first I meet up to see the girls, (Leanne, Rochelle, Louise ect).

"Hey" I shout catching their attention, "Hey there little girl" Louise says laughing a bit.

"Um, okay" I roll my eyes.

"Lilac!" Nick appeared and was smiling, but then it turned into regret, "I'm so so sorry about Friday night, I didn't mean to, I don't know what came over me, please I really didn't I don't like you like that, I will never do anything like that again once again I'm so sorry" Nick said in one breath.

"Nick, it's fine, well kind of but I forgive you, I know you were under the influence of alcohol, so don't worry just next time don't drink as much" I said while rubbing his arm lightly then walking over to Rochelle.

"Hey" I say while smiling, "Hello hello hellooo" Rochelle sung making me do the confused face.

"Sorry, I'm just really happy" she stated, "Why?" I ask but giggling at her.

"Okay don't blame me, but Luca asked me out on a date!" she squeaked, "Wow! Congrats!" I say while jumping up and down with her, "Let's go to my brother" she says so I nod and we head towards him.

"Do you think Luca is you're mate?" I ask, "I think so, but for some reason he isn't wolf, he is human, I can tell, so he won't feel the pull of our connection" she frowned.

"Trust me, he can feel the connection he just doesn't know what it means, I can sense he has strong feelings for you" I smirk, "Really?" she beamed, "Yes! Trust me, so just give him time and when the time comes we will tell him" I say which she nodded to.

We finally arrived where Blake was and I immediately hugged him snuggling my head on his back.

He hugged me back, my wolf purred, "Kiss him now, come on!" she begged, I just rolled my eyes, and pecked his lips.

"You gave into you're wolf?" Blake smirked, "Well she wanted a full on kiss, but a peck will have to do" I smile back.

Blake grins at me then pulls me by my waist and crashes his lips onto mine.

We make out for like five minutes then stop, we stare into each others eyes, and let me tell you, his beautiful eyes, you could get lost in them.

I smiled then pulled away, "Blake there is something you need to know" I start of, "What's wrong?" he asks.

"Willow, she had a vision, she saw someone killing her, she will die and we don't know when where who or why" I state with tears in my eyes.

"What? Why? What can I do?" Blake asks, "I don't know, but all I know is that, if Willow saw it, then it means it is by something supernatural" I said, "How was she killed?" Blake asks, "I- I don't know" I say,

The day goes by, and me ans Blake goes home so we can see Willow, "Willow come here now!" I say through mind link which Willow replies saying yes.

Willow walks through the door and hugs me, "Show us it again please" I ask, Willow nods and puts her hand on my cheek showing me her vision.

Vision:

"Willow where is she?" the man with dark hair said,

"You're not going to get her!" Willow snaps back, while using her wind power pushing him back,

"We will find her, for now, you can send her a message!" the man yells.

"Oh and what would that be?" Willow scoffs,

"This" he says and next thing we know, he looks into her eyes, Willow's bones start to crush, her spine is split, she is in pain, her blood is flowing out of her.

She screams in pain, the man smirks, Willow screams one last time before her neck is snapped.

End of Vision.

My eyes are watering, I look at Blake who also has sadness in his eyes, he saw the vision to.

"What was it that killed her?" Blake asked, "I don't know, but for some reason I feel the only way we will find out is if we talk to the dead" I reply, "You mean a ghost?" Blake asks, "No she doesn't she means, someone dead but still walks on the earth. A vampire" Willow corrects.

I nod, Blake frowns, "No absolutely not!", then I frown, "Blake, I'm going to talk to a vampire with or without you're permission, if it means I can save my sister then I am going to do it!" I snap.

Blake nods slowly, "I'm going to go home now" Blake states then leaves without another word.

"I'm sorry Lilac" Willow said, "For what?" I ask, "For causing you this trouble" she sighs, "No Willow, I need to know okay, I refuse to let you die!" I said while pulling her into a hug.

That night, I had no dinner and went straight to bed, I miss Blake already, and now he is annoyed with me I don't know what to do.

Even my wolf is complaining, all she keeps saying is "Mate, mate, go to mate, need mate, mate, MAAATTEEEE" Which is getting quite annoying.

Suddenly I heard my door open, and there he was, Blake.

"You're sister let me in, I'm so sorry, I miss you!" he states while walking over to me and hugging me while I'm on the bed.

I hug him back, "I miss you to" I whisper.

We pull back and stare into each others eyes, and both lean in.

We crash our lips together, he licks at my lower lip asking for entrance which I immediately grant, the kiss becomes more heated.

Blake then lays on top of me, then started to kiss down my neck, he found my soft spot and started to suck on it, I moan quietly, I can feel him smirk.

"Lilac, can I mark you?" Blake asks, I wasn't thinking, "Yes!" and I don't regret it.

He starts kissing my soft pot again, and soon bit down, there was pain for a few seconds but it turned into pure blissful pleasure.

I moan more, and start to play with his hair which he grunts to.

I wrap my legs around his waist pulling him closer to me, I then start grinding on him, we both moan in pleasure.

Blake started to rub my thigh, which made me sigh.

He starts to kiss me again, which also got heated again.

My arms are around his neck, I then slowly take of his top which he repeats by taking of mine, I scratch his back earning a moan from him.

He then takes of my shorts, and I take of his trousers, leaving us in our underwear.

I grind against him again, making us moan more.

"Are you sure about this?" Blake asks, "Yes!" I said and kiss him again.

He first takes of my bra, and starts to suck on my nipple, I moan again and play with his hair.

He then pulls of my underwear along with his, and without hesitation he pushes himself inside me, I thrown my head back and moan, trying not to be to loud which is good, because no one will hear as my room is sound proof.

Blake moans along with me and we start kissing again.

He thrusts in me, and let me say this, he is big!

Our moans fill the room, I pull him further inside me and moan louder, I was about to cum, "Hold it for a little longer babe" Blake says, I nod and let him thrust in me longer, until we both came and fell on my bed in each others arms.

"Wow" was all I could say, "Yes you were!" Blake states while snuggling into my neck, I put the blanket over us and we lay there cuddling in silence.

"Night babe" Blake whispers then kisses my for head, "Night night" I whisper back then cuddle back into him then slowly I fell asleep.

Chapter 14

Next day

My alarm goes of again in the morning, Blake is still here, "Blake get up" I say while nudging him.

He slowly opens his eyes then smiles, "Hey beautiful", I blush then get up to take a shower, I hear a growl then look and Blake who has lust in his eyes, then I realize, I'm still naked.

I smirk then walk into my bathroom keeping the door open.

The water flows down my body, I wash my hair and myself, then I feel hands on my waist.

I turn around to see Blake naked and in the shower with me.

We both smile then start to have a passionate kiss.

I wrap my arms around his neck and does the same around my waist.

He then starts to suck on my mark making me moan in pleasure.

After we finished our shower (After we did the deed) we got out and dried ourselves, I then dried my hair, and chose to wear light blue skinny jeans, with brown boots, and a red tank top, along with my black leather jacket.

I did my usual make up and as I finished I see that so was Blake, "I brought clothes with me" he told me, I nod, "Let's go" I say then we walk downstairs hand in hand.

We walk into the kitchen and have a slice of toast each, and then left in Blake's car.

We arrive at school, and then walk to the group, I see Elliot and smile, "Hello!" he said, "Hey" I say back then cuddle into Blake's side.

Elliot looks at Blake and smirks, "Any way, Blake where are the vampires?" I ask, Blake and Elliot look at me, "Blake don't look at me like that, I need to find them" I roll my eyes.

I then sensed them, I looked around to see their group, without hesitation I run up to them.

They look at me weirdly, "What do you want wolf?" a blond haired one spoke, "I need to ask you something" I snap, "I think you can help me" I explained further.

"Why would we help you?" said the same boy I saw yester-day, "I don't know, but I just have a feeling you can help me" I say back, "What do you need then?" he asks.

I walk closer to him, I then put my hand on his cheek showing him the vision that Willow sent me.

After he saw it he looked at me surprised, "You're the one?" was all he said "What?" I ask.

"You're the one they want, you're the mixed one" he said.

"Care to elaborate?" I ask still confused, "The hunters, they want you, they want you're powers, they want to use them against us all" he speaks, "THEY WILL NOT HAVE YOU!" he shouts.

"I'm confused" I said, "Hunters, they want to get you're powers so they ca kill us all, vampires, were wolfs, witches everything supernatural. We will help you okay, they will not get you okay, we join you, that is if you're mate and the others except us" he said.

I looked behind me, and indicated the group to come over.

All Blake, Rochelle, Cole, Leon, Noah and Elliot walk over, "They know what they are, they want to help, only if you except them" I said.

Blake growled, I looked at him, "Blake I know you hate vampires and I know why, but I need to save my sister, and all of you, they want to kill me, to kill you, I am not letting you die" I stare at Blake to see his reaction.

He soon relaxes the finally nods, "Fine, but if they lay one fang on you, their dead" Blake says firmly, "Dude, we're already dead" one vampire said, Blake just rolled his eyes.

"Okay, well we meet at the park after school, okay we will then head to the woods" I say, everyone nods.

So basically the day goes by, boring except when I'm wish Blake, but all I can think is, is Willow, I just don't want anything bad happening to her.

Finally the day ends, and I literally run home to get changed, then run to the park.

When I get to the park, I see all the vampires there, "Hey, I just noticed, I still don't know you're names" I ask, The one who I say first, with black hair spoke first, "I'm Liam", then the blonde one spoke, "I'm Charlie", then the next boy who had light brown hair spoke, "Ryan" then last the boy with light brown hair spoke, "Alex".

I nod, "Okay good to know" and after I said that I could smell my mate, it brought a smile to my face as I turn around to see him smiling back at me.

"Where is Willow?" he asks, "Does she need to be here?" I ask, "Yes" Blake replies, I nod.

"Willow, are you alone?" I ask, "Yeah, why?" he asks back, "Good, I'm calling for you okay, come here" I said, "Okay then" she said back.

I nod again, then I call for Willow, and then she appears in front of me, I smile then hug her.

"They are the vampires?" she asks while eyeing them, I just nod, "Thought so, I can smell the death on them" she smirks.

"Offensive" Charlie chuckled.

"Come on let's go" I say and we all head to the woods.

"Lilac, can you sense that?" Willow asks, "Yeah, I can" I say back.

"Sense what?" Blake asks.

"Death" was all I said.

Chapter 15

I start to walk faster finding where the sense was coming from, until I found a little boy, he was very pale, and black hair, he looks about ten.

I then hear a gasp, it was Liam, "That's my brother" Liam whispered.

I also hear Willow gasp, "Lilac, what is happening?" she asks, I can see the panic in her eyes, "What do you mean?" I ask.

"I can feel something, my heart, I can smell something amazing, yet, it smells like death" she states.

My eyes widen, "I think you're a wolf to, and you smell something amazing, which could be you're mate, and you smell death, and this boy is" I explain mostly to myself.

"Are you saying her mate is my brother?" Liam questions, I nod slowly.

"But he is dead?" Blake said, Willow's eyes water, "NO!" she screamed, then she looked confused.

"What the hell is going on?" she cries, "Okay can we try and help my brother please" Liam asks.

I nod, "We can't bring back dead to be dead, we can only bring them back to life" I said, "What does that mean?" Liam asks, "There is a big chance he will come back as a human" I explain.

Liam nods, "Willow help me" I suggest, she nods and sits on the other side next to him.

We put our hands on his heart, closing our eyes, I can feel the power coming out of me, and growing inside the boy.

I slight heart beat appears.

My eyes flutter open, I know they are a different colour now, most likely black as that is what happens when I use this kind of magic.

We both pull away and gasp for breath, as the boy shoots up also breathing like us.

"What is going on?" he cries clearly panicking.

"Trey!" Liam prays embracing him into a hug, "Dude, you're alive" Liam laughs, "What?! YES!" Trey screams, I look confused, well actually we all do.

Trey then looks at me and Willow, he smiles at Willow though, "Thank you" he said, I just smile and nod, where as Willow actually hugged him, and he hugged her back.

I giggled slightly, "Somebody's in love" I said through mind link, Willow groaned then pulled away shooting me daggers.

This time I burst out laughing where as everyone else looks at me confused, except from Blake who has an amused look.

"Kiss mate! Dude do it!!" my wolf commanded, I just rolled my eyes, where as Blake must of sensed what my wolf said as he smirked then gave me a quick peck on my lips.

"So Trey, can you tell me how you died? You know again?" Liam asked Trey.

"Hunters, they caught me of guard, I was feeding and they just appeared, then killed me" Trey answered but he was looking as Willow, and Willow was staring at him, smiling.

I rolled my eyes again, "Those damn hunters, they are getting better" Charlie said.

"So, can someone now tell me, why do they actually want me? And how do they know about me?" I ask.

The vampires look at me, Liam was the only one to speak, "They know about you because of you're ancestors were witches, and they made a spell that would make every generation stronger, and then wolves joined you're family, making you stronger and faster. Then when you're grandmother turned you're age she had new powers that no other witch had, because of the wolf, and then she made a spell, that her next generation of first born girls would be stronger than witches, wolfs, vampires and much more supernatural creatures, but she only had you're father, so when he had children we had to wait for their first born girl, which was you and because you're mother was a full wolf, you have got that extra wolf inside you. Now the hunters want you because they know you are connected to supernaturals by blood and magic, and I don't know this but they somehow think they can use you to kill all supernaturals" Liam wasn't even out of breath as he said this.

My eyes were wide open, in fear, confusion and fantasized.

"So you're saying, if the hunters got me, they would use me to kill all of you?" I ask, they all nod, I then got scared and was pulled into a hg by Blake.

My wolf purred, even though I didn't see but I can tell Blake is smirking.

"What can we do then?" Blake asked suddenly all serious.

"We have to kill the hunters, there arn't many but they are hard to find" Charlie responded while the other vampires nod in agreement.

"How do we do that then?" Blake replies with a sarcastic tone.

The vampires looked at me, I nodded.

"I have to lead them to me, then they will most likely be more of them, the more there are, the more we kill" I say bluntly.

"Hell no, over my 30 inch dic-" I cut him of.

"Stop it idiot, okay we need to do this, I am safe as well, you know the senses I have, if they are near I will sense them easily" I replied while smirking.

I can tell he wasn't happy with this but hey what you going to do?

"How do we get them to come after you?" Rochelle asks, I think for a while.

Then I look at the vampires, "The only way I can think of is if you are at the scene of a lot of supernatural attacks, then they will look around, and when they see you, they will have to see you attack as well though, which means using you're magic" Liam answered.

I nod, "When do we do this?" I ask, Blake is glaring at me, "Are you going to attack an innocent?!" he raised his voice a little making me flinch.

"Yes Blake, if it means killing the hunters then Yes, plus I won't need to do much, I can use my powers to sense them, plus I wont hurt them much, and after I will heal the innocent" I explain.

Blake finally gives in and nods.

"Willow, come with me quickly" I say, Willow nods and follows me.

I create a circle so no one can hear us, "Lilac what's up?" Willow asks.

"If the hunters want me, and they want to use me to kill the supernaturals, I can't just sit around and attack innocents until they find me, I need to find them first, but I need you're help, and Trey's" I explain.

"What can Trey do?" Willow asks curiously, "He was killed by a hunter, I know what to do, but I need you're help to get the information, he's you're mate. You're connection will be stronger than mine" I explain more.

"Okay then, what do we do?" she asks, "First we leave, but we must get Trey, only for a while, so I can get the information needed" I said.

"What are you going to do?" Willow questions, I pause for a moment.

"I'm going to tap into all my powers, then I'm going for a journey, in his past"....

Chapter 16

N ext Day.

Basically what happened after mine and Willows conversation, we all left, and I told Willow to ask Trey if he can come round, and he said yes, but then Liam butted in and said he is coming as well, since Trey is no longer a vampire.

"When is he here?" I ask Willow, "Now" she replied at the doorbell went of.

We walked to the door and let both Trey and Liam to come in.

They entered and sat on the sofas in the lounge.

"Trey, there is something I need to ask you" I start of, Trey nodded back.

Hey just realized, he is actually 10 years old, ha! He acts older.

"I need to go inside you're mind, I will tap into my powers, that most likely haven't been used, and I will go inside you're mind" I said.

"Why?" was all he said, "Because then I can see all the hunters you have seen, and then I can send it to Willow, where she will then have to sense either the same person, or a relative, that way we find the hunters" I explain.

"Wait, I thought we were waiting for them to come to us?" Liam asked, "I'm not waiting" I snap.

"Okay, do it" Trey finally answered.

So I sat next to him, I took a long breath, "Willow get me a knife please" I ask, instantly both Trey and Liam freeze, "Why?" Trey asks worried, "I need you're blood" I reply back.

Willow comes back with a knife, I then cut Treys hand, then mine, and then blend them together by holding his hand.

I say the spell in my head, and instantly fall asleep....

Treys Past

It was all happening fast, as I was forwarding the past to get to what happened before he died again.

I saw many many deaths.

Then one memory of Trey's caught my attention.

It was my grandmother, she knew Trey?

I watched what was happening, Liam was also there, my grandma must of been around 27 or 30, "Please, make sure you will keep my first born girl safe, even if she isn't mine, the first born girl in my family in the next generation, just please keep her safe, she will need it." My grandma said strongly.

Both Trey and Liam nod before disappearing.

I'm forwarding again, it feels like hours until I am finally at the time I want to be at.

Trey is feeding on a deer.

Then I hear a sound, Trey turns around to see around 20 guys standing close to him, then they were all around him.

"What do you want hunters?" Trey snapped.

"The mixed one, we need her, and killing you is going to get her!" one man spat back.

"And how will that work out for you?" Trey asked sounding bored.

"We kill you, you're brother will find a witch, the mixed one, and she will bring you to life, we will know that she is here, and then we're coming for her." a different man coldly replied while staring at Trey like her is filth.

"So, what makes you think the witch will bring to to life again?" Trey scoffs, "We can only hope, but she won't be able to help it, it is her nature to help you're kind" the same man spat.

"Fine, then try to kill me if you can" Trey chuckles before turning around then ran at his full speed, he turned around to see if he was followed, no one was there, he smirked and turned around.

He was then stabbed in his heart with a wooden stake, it is a women that stabbed him, "Cold dirt!" she spat before Trey fell to the floor dead.

End Of Trey's past

I wake up gasping for air, my heart is racing, and I'm all sweaty, and let me tell you something, I have a huge headache, I feel like I'm going to be sick, I think my nose is bleeding, I feel weak and I might pass out, eh I guess this is what happens when you use magic you force to use, and also magic that shoudln't be used.

"Lilac, oh my God, are you okay?" Willow asks as she walks over to my hugging me, "I- I um Fee- I, Ca-" I kept stuttering, I couldn't really speak.

"Call for blake" I say through mind link to Willow, she nods to me and calls him to come over our house.

I sit there for a few minutes when the door crashes open and a very worried looking Blake stands there scanning the room until he found me then ran over t me, "Babe what happened, what's wrong, why is you're wolf crying? What happened?" Blake questions.

I gesture over to Willow in hope she would explain, "She tapped into power that shouldn't be used unless practiced which she didn't do, so she can see through Trey's past to see who the hunters were" Willow explained.

Blake looked confused for a second, then annoyed.

"Why?" he growled immediately sending me an apologetic look.

"So she can find the hunters" Willow replied using a 'duh' tone.

Blake rolled his eyes, "S-sorry" I chocked out, Blake immediately hugged me, "It's okay baby" he hushed.

Chapter 17

I then fell asleep leaning on Blake's shoulder.

I then wake up, I don't know how long I was out but now I feel refreshed and better.

Willow, I must find her!

I was trying to sense her when I realized I was in my room, hmm, okay.

I sensed both Blake and Willow downstairs so I walked down there and smiled.

"Hey, are you better now?" Willow asked, I nodded, "I'm sending you the memories" I said and sent Willow all the hunters I saw, Willow nodded and sat down as her magic to her into her own world.

"What is she doing?" Blake asked, "I sent her the hunters, one of her gifts is to find either the same person or a relative, I don't really know how it works but yeah" I explain.

"Oh, well will it work though?" Blake asked me, "It usually does, we have practiced things like this sort of, well not the whole going in someones mind and their past but like tracking people, but only people from not that far so this is pretty advanced for us" I sigh.

"What will happen this? Will the same thing happen to Willow?" Blake asks concerned, "No, the magic I did, is a really strong magic, and you are supposed to gradually build it up to do what I did, but I just forced it, which is why all this happened to me" I explain which Blake nodded to.

"But Lilac, please don't do that again, if you want to then please just practise I don't want anything else happening to you" Blake whispered while he pulled me into a hug, I think he was actually sniffing me, wolf thing?

I took a long loud breath and then sat down waiting for Willow to come back.

"Want a drink?" Blake asks, "Tea please?" I said looking up giving him my 'wolf' (puppy) eyes, (See what I did there?), he chuckled and nodded giving me a kiss on my forehead then heading out.

I sat there looking at Willow, "Willow?" I called out through mind link to make sure she is okay.

As I was listening inside her head for a reply, I heard a few 'mhm's' which basically means 'hey, busy so shut up and let me continue' so I took the hint and shut up.

I was a bit bored so I decided to do some spells, only small indoor ones though, not the spells that will either 'accidently' blow my house up, or 'RUIN MY HAIR' - said in a high pitch girly scream.

I chuckled to myself then shook my head at the thought.

I decided to do some movement spells, so I basically said one spell and now I can move anything, in any way.

I moved the other sofa towards the door so when Blake comes back he should be like 'What the heck?'.

Then I moved MYSELF, up to the ceiling so he won't see me, then I did a mind trick, basically tricking the mind to I made the room 'look' like a room full on snakes, and the sofa is covered in them.

God Blake's face will be classic, in fact, I might make myself look like a huge snake and try to 'kiss' him, but it will look like I'm trying to bite him.

Eventually Blake cam back but dropped my tea at the sight! NO MY TEA!

He was looking around as if trying to think either where to escape or where I am.

I jumped down, looking like a snake in his eyes, he looked at me panicked.

I got closer until I was in front of him, about to kiss him, and then boom!

I kissed him, his eyes open still and at that moment everything went back to normal.

His eyes widened, "What the? What was all that?!" Blake exclaimed, I just laughed, "The good old mind trick" I laughed again but stopped.

"My poor tea!" I cried, well not literally but yeah.

Blake rolled his eyes, "Uh sista that would nut of happen if you dint scure moi lik dat!" Blake spoke in a gay, chavy, slang, once again gay way.

I just looked amused, "Nice, no wonder we are made for eachutha!" I laughed which Blake soon joined.

We both stopped as we heard a loud breath, I looked and saw Willow has awoken and is panting.

I ran over to her, "Are you okay?" I said worried.

"Water, need water" she whispers.

I use my magic to make a glass of fresh water appear and then gave it to her.

"Thanks" she says with a normal voice, "Okay so what happened?" I ask.

I didn't find all of them, but most of them" she answers, "why did you take so long though?" I question, "I couldn't find that cow who actually killed my Trey! So I took my time until I finally found her daughter, and her husband! But not her so I guess we get her by her loved ones" Willow explained, I nod, "Okay well we will start tomorrow!" I announce.

"Princess what about school? You can't miss a lot of days when you first started" Blake complains, "Blake, I need to, I'd rather have no education and save my sister and all of our kinds, than learn about stuff I don't need and in the end we all die, so yes I can" I snap back, my wolf whimpers obviously not wanting to fight with her mate, "Look I'm sorry Blake it's just I can't lose you" I say more kinder and then hug him.

"I don't want to lose you either" Blake whispered in my ear.

"Then let me save you all" I whisper back.

He let out a loud sigh, "Fine, but I'm going with you and as many people who will help us okay, there is no way you are going on you're own!" Blake insists, I just roll my eyes and nod the smile.

Okay well it is late so I started to head to bed. "BEDTIME!" I call out.

Willow went to her room and Blake went with me to my room.

I got changed into a baggy top and underwear then jumped on my bed where Blake joined my topless and only in boxers.

I cuddled up to him, "Hey where is everyone else? Luke mum dad, brothers?" I ask actually not knowing, "You're mum and dad are out on a romantic night out, and you're brothers are out at some party." Blake explained, "Oooh" I yawned, "Go to sleep princess" Blake insists.

"Night" I whisper, "Good night me beauty" he whispered back kissing my forehead which made me smile, then slowly fall asleep.

Chapter 18

I woke up the next morning in Blake's arms, I smile but then realized I need to get ready, I sigh and get up.

I have a shower then got changed into my black skinny jeans, black tank top and black leather jacket and black boots, yeah I may have a heat stroke but hey I need to wear this for what I am going to do today. I walk out of the bathroom after doing my makeup and saw that Blake wasn't in bed, but I could smell bacon and eggs!

I sprinted down the stairs to the kitchen to see my family sitting down as Blake is serving, "I must say Lilac, he's a keeper" Mum nodded in approval while smirking, I nod back.

"Mhm, I'm going to have to agree with that" dad also smirked as he dug in. I just let out a slight laugh then sat down, "Princess what are you wearing?" Blake asks me, "AW!" mum shouts at Blake's comment, I blush.

"Clothes" I answer while rolling my eyes, "Nope, you are not wearing that outside! At all!" Blake ordered, "And why not?" I challenged, "First, you will die of heat, and I don't want you to be dead at all and secondly, you are mine beautiful, and no one else will look at you, but that will be hard if you wear that" Blake argued back, I let out a loud sigh, "Fine!" I sigh in defeat, "I will change" I moan the I trod up the stairs to my room but I hear my dad say "You know what, we can become quite good friends" once again I just roll my eyes.

I came back down after I changed into shorts that cover my bum, and a short dress top thing, with brown ankle boots.

I looked a Blake, then spun around giving him a look to see if it is okay.

"You could do better, but it will do" he smirked, I smirk back then hug him, "Sorry Lilac it's just well you're mine and I don't want anyone to think they can have you" Blake spoke sofly while kissing the top of my head, I smile then snuggle into his neck.

"It's okay, thank you" I speak quietly.

We break away from our hug and then head to find Willow.

She was in her room sitting down drawing, I looked around her room and smiled, her drawings are everywhere.

"Lilac!" Willow beamed and smiled, "Hey, we need to start to find the hunters now or something, where do we find them?" I ask.

"Okay well we are going to have to transport there, trust me it is the only easy way" Willow starts of, "Wait wait, 'WE'?!" I ask, she nods, "Lilac, I'm coming with you, okay two witches is stronger than one okay so get over it, plus you need me" Willow argues, "Fine!" I sigh frustrated.

"Blake get the wolfs and vampires!" I order, he nods and gets calls them.

After a while everyone was here, Cole, Elliot, Noah, Rochelle and Leon, and also the vampires, Liam, Charlie, Ryan and Alex.

We was about to leave when the door was opened, and there, was my parents and both my brothers.

"Where are you going missy?" my dad said in a sassy way, "Witch stuff" I reply, all their eyes widen and look at the company we have, "They all no, and mum I know I'm wolf, plus I found my mate, and if you smell something a bit of, well that would be the vampires, they are here because of witch stuff okay!" I explain.

"Lilac, no you're not, okay! Magic is hard you can't use it all the time!" my mum complained.

"I'm sorry" I whisper, I take a deep breath, "Sleep" I whisper to myself and with that my parents and brothers collapse on the ground sleeping.

"How long will they be out for?" Charlie asked me, "However long I want them to be" I smirk at him.

"Okay how do we get there?" Liam asked, "Magic" both me and Willow say in sync.

"Connect hands" I order, and that is what we do, we all create a huge circle, I'm holding Willow's and Blake's hand!

"I nod at Willow, she smiles, we both close our eyes, Willow sent me the location, and with that we transported to our first target.

Chapter 19

As I opened my eyes we were outside a cottage, I smile at how cute it was, "Let's go" Blake states, I stop him, "Blake no!" I start of, "Willow who are we looking for?" I ask, "Well I think it's their leader, I've looked them up and yeah I think she is" Willow explains, "How are actually going to do this? I mean we can't just get rid of the leader and they stop" Rochelle complains, "True" Willow agrees, "I have an idea but it will be hard, I was thinking we create a spell to bind all the hunters together, then we have a choice, kill them or to make them forget us" I suggest, "KILL!" Liam chooses, "Yeah, Lilac we can't make them forget, as much as I hate it, but we have to kill them" Blake informs me, "Fine" I whisper, I don't want to kill them, but if that's the only way to protect my kind then fine.

"How do we bind them?" Charlie asks, before I could answer Willow did, "We need more witches", I agreed with her, "So how do we find witches?" Blake asked.

"You don't we do" I tell him, "Willow send them back home, then let's go" I order Willow, she nods, and with that she sent everyone back home, "You know Blake will be pissed of right?" Willow smirks, "Yeah, but let's go" I smile at her and with that we disappeared to look for witches.

Chapter 20

It has been 4 weeks, I have been sending Blake stuff to make sure he knows I'm okay, turns out they are all back at school, but my family, well they are still asleep, as much as I find it amusing, it is better that way, and even though Rochelle wants me to bring her mate back I still refuse to because well, I can't, they will try and stop us, but we need to do this, I need to do this.

"Lilac, how many do we have now?" Willow asks me while searching for more witches, "So far I think 34 witches, some aren't very powerful, but still it's better for everyone if we have more" I answer Willow, "Okay good, we only need 6 more really, that shouldn't be too hard considering there is actually a circle in this area" Willow smirks, "Good, when should we go?" I ask, "Now, we need to hurry up and get back, plus we need to cast the spell to bind them, then we have to kill them, but hopefully this spell won't do this, it will just make them not exist, as if they never have, so if they had children they will be gone as well, and no one will remember them, they will be gone forever" Willow explained, I nod, "Good to know, now let's go" I say and with that we left to find the circle.

We found the circle in the middle of a forest in their small town, I walk up to them, and they stare at me shocked, "Leave now!" one of them snap, "Look, I'm sorry for interrupting you're circle, but I need 6 more witches, and you just so happen to have 6, you're most likely confused so I will introduce myself, I'm Lilac, and I'm a witch, but some supernaturals call me the 'mixed one'. I am known to be the most powerful witch, but sadly there are some people that want me, and all witches, wolfs, vampires all supernaturals dead, and they will by using me, so we need to stop them before they will us all, we already have 34 witches, including me and my sister, we just need 6 more, are you willing to help us?" I explain to them, they all look at each other shocked, "Yes, we will join you, if it means saving future generations, then yeah, we will help you" a young lady agreed while smiling.

"Thank you, now will you all link hands with us, and we will transport to the other witches, we will train you, and teach you the spell and then, Willow will send you who we will link together and we will go on from there" I explain, they all nod and link hands with each other, after that we transported to a huge hall that has been protected so no one will find or sense us.

1 week later

We finally are fully trained, and no what we are doing, "Lilac, what about the others?" Willow asked, "They don't need to help us" I answer back, "Link hands everyone!" I shout so everyone can hear me, they all obeyed and held hand creating a huge circle, I stood in the middle, "Now you all know you're training, Willow send who we are linking" I tell Willow, she nods and closes her eyes.

Everyone sees it, "You know what to do now!" I say to everyone, they all nod and do the spell to bind all the hunters together, now because the witches aren't very powerful, they are using some of my magic to make the spell stronger.

I could feel the energy being taken from me, it was like I was being drained, I was becoming weaker and weaker, it felt like they were doing this for hours, until finally my body couldn't take it, and then I passed out.

I then woke up in a bed, "Willow!" I called out, "I'm here don't worry" Willow turns up and sat beside me, "What happened?" I asked, "You fainted, because of the energy was being taken, so you grew weak, the spell worked though, they are all connected now, you just need to gain you're strength back, so we are going home!" Willow explains, I was too tired to argue so I agree and rest, slowly falling asleep again.

I woke up again, not in the same place as before, but in my room, I roll over and then see Blake asleep, I smile then cuddle into him, "Morning princess" he whispers, "Morning" I reply then look at him, "How long have I been asleep for?" I ask, "Well a day" he replies with a smirk, "Oh" I giggle.

"So what are we going to do now?" I ask, Blake looked a bit confused at first but then realized what I was on about, "Well they are all bounded, so now we just need to do the other spell thing, but not now, you need to gain you're strength back, you are quite weak according to Willow" Blake informs me, "Does she know what I should do?" I said, "You can't use you're magic at all for a little while" Blake explains, "Easier said than done" I laugh before cuddling back into Blake, "Don't worry, I know you will do it" Blake whispers then kisses my head while once again I fall back asleep

dream...

"Lilac?" a small voice whispered, I open my eyes to see a white background, everything is so bright, but soft, "Lilac?" the voice whispered again, "Who is it?" I ask, my voice is a lot more soft and pure right now.

"Lilac my dear, it's me" I look around to find the owner of the voice, and when I found the person, "Grandma?" I ask, "My dear, how are you?" she asks while walking towards me, "Okay? Wait, am I dead or something, or is this just a dream?" I ask, "It's a dream, but I have entered you're dream, I needed to talk to you and this was the only way I knew how" my grandma explained, I nod, "What did you want to talk to me about?" I ask.

Grandma then looked nervous, "Honey the hunters know you have bounded them, and they know you're weak, they are coming for you now! The only thing you can do is to do the spell, but I know you're weak" Grandma gave me a small sad smile, "What will happen? I'm too weak to do this, I might die!" I exclaim, "It's a risk you have to make I'm afraid" Grandma told me, "What do I do then?" I ask, Grandma's face became more serious, "You must pretend to be asleep so everyone will leave you, find one of the hunters and let them take you with them, they will think you're weak, and you won't do the spell alone, which you're not supposed to do, so they will consider you weak, powerless and vulnerable, but at the most unexpected time, you will need to cast the spell, take every ounce of power you have and you didn't know you had, to cast the spell" Grandma tells me, "Then what happens to me?" I ask regretting the thought, "That's up to fate what happens to you, you live or you join me" Grandma croaks out, "I'm so sorry, I never expected it to come to this" Grandma apologizes, "It's okay, after all, it is my fate" I realize, "Yes, but that doesn't make it fair" Grandma argued "Life isn't fair, and i'm just going to have to go along with it" I sigh, "Okay, but before you go, remember you can't tell anyone, not even you're mate"' Grandma orders, "Okay" I whisper, "bye Grandma, maybe I will see you soon" I whisper while tears escaped my eyes, "Goodbye sweetheart" grandma whispered back before I collapsed.

End of Dream..

I woke up panting and sweating, remembering the dream, well sort of a dream I just had, I look around to see it is night time, and Blake is sleeping, okay so I need to come up with a plan.

I thought different ideas until the best idea was so wait until either everyone is asleep, or until everyone is too busy to think of me so I can leave.

I decided now wouldn't be the best time as Blake would sense me, so I thought for a little while longer before resting my head and looking at Blake.

"You're seriously staring at me at this time?" Blake's husky voice whispered while I see a small smirk for on his mouth, "Yeah, just woke up and can't sleep" I admit, "Oh, well if you can't sleep then let's talk for a bit okay" Blake offered, "Yeah" I reply, so he then opened his eyes turned to face me then pulled me into his chest while playing with my hair.

"Do you still feel weak?" Blake asked with clear concern in his voice, "Yeah" I croak trying to fight back the tears, "You will be better don't worry, just don't use any magic at all and you will be fine in no time" Blake assured me, "Blake, my whole body feels weak, it feels like someone pushed me out a window, down some stairs and just beat the hell out of me, this pain, is just too hard to cope" I explain to him, "Lilac, don't worry, you will be fine, okay, the pain will go away" Blake tried to comfort me, it sort of worked but I still know that I can't stay like this.

"Lilac, let's sleep now, you need you're energy" Blake told me, "Okay" I whisper before cuddling into his chest and then slowly falling asleep.

I woke up the next day and looked around to see Blake wasn't here, I smile then slowly get up, I thought that if I leave then Blake will be able to sense me, so I then masked my scent, it doesn't take being a witch to do this, so I masked my wolf scent to they won't be able to find me, I then slowly get up and and then go to the window, but I quickly stopped to quickly write a letter to everyone saying,]

"Please don't look for me, I have left, I really can't handle this anymore, I'm leaving for a while, being here just reminds me of magic and I need to get away from it all, I love you all, I will be back. maybe

Love Lilac xxxxx

I put it on the bed then slowly climb out the window being as quiet as possible so they won't hear me, and as I drop to the ground I get and and start to walk away from the house, now I just need to think, if I was a hunter where would I be?

The day went on from me walking around, but far away from home so they won't find me, Willow has tried to mind link me but I refused to let her in, I've even blocked out my wolf, which is quite hard.

I am still very wear, and now very hungry since I don't actually remember the last time I ate anything, but I continue walking hoping a hunter would be around and would recognize who I am, but so far no luck.

It was really dark now, I don't know what time it is either, but I do know that I am just walking along a rode to wherever, but that doesn't stop me.

Cars drive past ignoring me until one car stops, a women comes out, and I immediately recognize her, she smirks at me, "What are you doing out here all alone?" she asks while still smirking, "I got lost" i lie pretending I don't know she is a hunter, "Come with me, I will take you home" she smiles evilly, "Okay" I whisper before she helps me into her car, and as I was about to get in she hit a hard object around my head making my vision go blurry until it then turned blank...

I wake up in a small room tied onto a chair, "Wakey wakey" A harsh voice spoke, I look around to see three people, two men and one girl.

"Looks like you're out of luck, it's a pleasure to finally meet the one and only mixed one" one of them men spoke while smirking, "You too" I smirk back, "Looks like we're going to have fun now" the other man spoke, "Shut up you two! Call the leader we need everything prepared!" the girl snapped, she then looked at me and smirked then walked towards me slowly until she was right in front of me, "No one can find

you anymore, and if they do, it will be too late, soon you're
pathetic kind will all die!".

Chapter 21

I stare at them blankly, they clearly were not happy as they expected me to be scared, "I know you know I'm weak, and you're in luck, I don't want them to find me" I laugh, "Why the hell not?" the first man spat, "Because I know that you will hurt or kill them" I snap back, "Fair enough" he smirked.

"Look, not to break you're conversation, but like I said call the boss! She needs to get here now, we can't risk her gaining strength, so the more time you waist, the stronger she can get!" the girl hissed, both men nod eagerly and scurried off.

"Tell me something, why did you leave unprotected?" the girl smirked, "I honestly don't know, but can you tell me, why do you all think I can help kill all supernaturals?" I ask, she looks a bit taken back at first, "We don't assume, we know!" she snaps, "Yes, but how? What can I do?" I push, "I'm not telling you anything! If you want to know ask the boss! And she will tell you if she wants okay!" she yells, I smile then nod slowly.

"So, when will you're 'boss' be here? I feel like a chat" I smirk, "Soon" was all the girl said, I nod while breathing in loudly.

We sat, well I sat she stood, there for a good half an hour until the two men came back in, "The boss is here" one of them tells the girl, she quickly nods before smirking at me before leaving the room, so I was alone...

After like another five minutes someone entered the room, it was a tall brunette women, most likely in her early thirties, "You the boss?" I ask without hesitation, "Yes, I am, and you're the mixed one, am I correct?" she asked while standing there, "Yeah, but most people call me Lilac" I laugh fakely, she glares at me, "Good to know" she said.

"Now down to business, we need you, and I know you won't do what we say willingly, so we will let you live as long as you give me you're powers, then I will use the magic to kill all supernaturals, and I know you will never do the spell, so give it to me" she explains, "Um, sorry, but it is my power, so no, you're not getting them!" I snap, "Besides, if I do, YOU will be supernatural, thus killing yourself... Now isn't that a stupid thing to do now? Or is suicide you're best choice now?" I smirk, "I'm willing to die as long as it means you're kinds die along!" she hissed before slapping me, "Now, give me you're magic, or we will torture you slowly, and painfully!" she threatened, "Go for it!" I dare, she smirks before pulling out a butterfly knife cutting my cheek, it was painful, but I tried my best not to show any emotion.

She clearly didn't like this so she stabbed my left leg three times, the pain was unbearable, I knew I can't give in, so I took all the pain that was coming my way...

A couple of hours later, let's say I'm bleeding a lot now, but one of there doctors stitched me up, and some stuff to make sure I don't get infected as they want to hurt me, not an infection, so here I am, all achy as they gave me nothing for the pain.

I am back in the room I was in before, nothing but my blood on the floor as they didn't clean it up, then someone entered, "Since you refuse to give in, we will torture you any ways possible, so now, you can starve!" they laugh before leaving me there.

I have no Idea how long I have been here for, but it felt like years, but I know if must of only been like a couple days or something like that, but let me tell you this all they would give me for food is a slice of bread to last me for the day, then a different man would come in to beat me up, then the boss comes in every now and then to see if I have given in, but of course I refuse to which would result in being stabbed or cut again...

More and more days passed, I have no idea what to do now, I have been beaten up daily, stabbed almost everyday, fed close to nothing but yet I still don't give in, I think it is because I'm a very stubborn person but let's just say right now I hate it.

"So, are you going to give in? Or do we have to tab and beat you to death?" a voice spat, I turn around slowly as my body ached, I feel so weak, much weaker than before, but I have to let my magic grow, so the weaker they make me the more they think they will win, but they have another thing coming...

I ignore her, mainly because I don't really have the strength to speak, I think she knew that so she carried on speaking, "Look, just give in, you won't have to go through all of this, or do you like being tortured? If I were you I would just give in before we kill you" she said attempting to be nice but I can see the irritation in her eyes..

I couldn't speak so I just ignored her and closed my eyes afraid that tears will fall showing her how weak I am, but I won't show her it, I won't give her the satisfaction.

"Fine, you just made your grave" she snapped before walking of, I don't know what she will do now, but I know it will hurt, all I want now is for her to leave me alone, and everyone, but I doubt that will happen..

A few hours have gone by, and no one has bothered me, I'm also gaining strength, but I'm still not strong enough to do any magic, at lease I don't think I do..

At that moment someone barged through the door, I look at who it is and my eyes widen.

Chapter 22

I can't believe he's here.. "W-what, a-are, you, do-doing, he-here?" I ask, with every word in pain and agony. He looked at me with a pained expression, "To fucking save you!" he whisper-shouted, he then slowly walked over to me, "What have they done to you?" he whispered while stroking my cheek softly. Tears start to form, "How, d'ya. Get, h-here?" I stutter, "I have my ways. I never stopped. I couldn't sleep, eat, or anything, I just needed to get you back, and then we found this dude, and well threatened his family, so he told us where you were, and got us in" Blake explained with a smirk.

I smile, then he slowly leans in and gives me a soft passionate kiss, making sure not to hurt me, tears fell down my cheeks. During this moment, I finish the spell to get rid of all hunters. I slowly got weaker and weaker as the spell continued. As the spell came to an end, my vision got darker, and darker, I became weaker. Then everything went black.

Chapter 23

Dream...

I hear laughter, everything is bright. I'm on a hill, beautiful green grass, the warm sun, flowers, birds, everything is perfect. Where am I? I look around and see people, lot's of people. Some laying down relaxing, some smiling and playing. Someone was walking up to me..

"Grandma?" I whisper as I take in who I see, "Yes, it is me" grandma smiles, my eyes start watering, "Grandma, oh my God, I missed you so much!" I cry while pulling her into a hug. "Lilac my dear, why are you here?" she whispered, I look at her confused, "Where?" I ask, "Lilac, you're in supernatural heaven" she informed, "Why am I here?" I ask, "I don't know sweetheart" Grandma said, "Am. Am I dead!?" I screeched, tears fell down my cheeks, "No no no nonononoonono!" Grandma stopped me, "Lilac, calm down" "I can't calm down! I fucking dead! What the? I- I'm so confused!" I scream as I begun to panic, "Lilac, please, calm down" Grandma tried to sooth, but then someone appeared, grandma bowed, "Lilac, I'm the moon Goddess, I heard what is happening, and I thought you would like to know. You are not dead" she spoke softly, I placed my hand over my heart, "Thank God, but why am I here?" I ask, "Well, it seems that you are nearly dead, I'm afraid. You see doing the spell when you were weak, physically as well as magically, and well because of that, you went into some sort of shock, and well now you're in a coma, and because you're a very powerful witch you have seemed to some how come here" she explained.

"So, what happens from here?" I ask, "Nothing I'm afraid, we can't change anything, it is against our nature to fix something that is dead. Only people below can help now, up here we can only watch." she explained, "Do we just stay here? Or can we go anywhere else?" I ask, "Sorry, but unless they call for you, we have to stay here, well only if you're new to death, if you have been here a while, well you develop a power to see what is happening with loved ones" grandma explained, "Oh" I whisper..

"So, what do I do now grandma?" I ask, "Nothing honey" she said with a sad face, I nod, "Okay". I then start to walk away, it is rather beautiful here, but I really can't. I have this strong pain in my chest, I don't know what it is though. "It's me" my wolf spoke, "What?" I ask her, "We're dead, and well, I can feel Blake's heart break, he is in pain, and we can feel it because we're not really dead yet" my wolf managed to choke out. "You don't think he will. Do anything stupid do you?" I ask her, "'God I pray he doesn't" she whispered clearly heart broken.

Tears welled in my eyes and started falling, I miss Blake so much, I miss mum, dad, Luca, Riley, and especially Willow, I miss everyone, I just want to go back! I don't want to have to suffer this heart break. How long am I going to be feeling this! "Lilac?" a voice appeared, I turn around and become shocked. "Granddad?" I whisper, he smiles and I run up to him then hug him, "I haven't seen you since you were five my dear" he said while kissing my cheek, "I know" I whisper, of the memory because he died of cancer.. "Wow, you have grown up into a beautiful young lady, but why the tears?" he asked with concern then his face came to realization, "Oh yeah, you're here, which means you're dead!? Honey what happened?" he asked with tears in his eyes, "That's one reason, I miss my mate Granddad!, I miss him so much!" I cried as he pulled me into a hug, "Oh sweetie, tell me what happened" he said, I nod, "I did a spell that went wrong, and now I've been told I'm in a coma, and I'm not dead, but not alive" I explain, "There is a way I can help you?" he suggested, I nod, "Like what?" I ask, "I've been here a long time, I can look at my loved ones, your family?" he said, I nod eagerly, "Please".

He nods then freezes. I look at him confused, then he takes my hand and I see Willow. My mum, dad, brothers, but no Blake. They are all in a hospital room and I'm laying there, emotionless, like a corpse. "Come back. Come back. Come back" Willow whispered over and over. I start crying again as we come back to where I am. granddad smiles softly, "Where's grandma?" I ask, "With the moon Goddess dear" he explained, "Oh" I whisper. "Honey, I have to go but I will be back very soon, I promise" granddad told me, I nodded then walked away and sat alone.

I start crying again and my wolf joins in, "Is this what it is like? I thought if you die, you wouldn't feel anything, hell I was wrong" I tell my wolf, and she agrees. "Lilac" a soft voice called, and I turned around and saw the Moon Goddess, I stood up and quickly bowed."Yes?" I ask politely."Come walk with me" she said, so I quickly walk up to her and we start walking around. "So, how are you feeling?" she asks, "Honestly? I feel like crap" I admit, she giggles, "Yeah, you will at first" she said, "What about this heart break? How long will this last?" I ask, "That all depends on you" she answered, "What does that mean?" I ask confused, "It means I don't know, only you can stop the pain. You're the one who won't let go, and with not letting go, you're holding onto all the pain, and well the longer you carry it around, the harder it gets" she explained, "'So you're saying, i need to let go of the pain?" I ask, she nods, "But, I can't" I whisper ashamed, "I know" she sighed.

"I must go now, lovely to chat, good bye Lilac" she smiled while disappearing. I honestly don't know what to do now. I'm feeling so many emotions, shocked, hurt, pain, scared. What am I supposed to do now?

Chapter 24

Willow's POV:

It's been a month and Lilac is still in a coma, I still haven't slept, then again, no one has, I just keep praying she will wake up, but I know that it won't happen, not anymore, I'm loosing all hope. "Willow, please eat something" my mum asked once again, "No, I don't want to eat, I don't deserve food!" I snap, "Please honey, this isn't your fault" dad tried to help but it didn't, I just ignored them both, they sighed then sat back down on their seats next to Lilac's bed, we are at the hospital.

"Mum, I'm going to go home" I quickly say while standing up, "I will take ou" dad said, "No, I will get Blake to, I will be back, don't worry" I say while walking out to find Blake. As I spotted him I went to him, "Blake take me home now!" I demand, he looked shocked, "For a little girl you sure are demanding" he smirked, "Innocent" I fake smirked, "Seriously now!" I say then start walking out of the hospital with him closely behind and we head over to his car. "Why are we going to your house?" Blake asked, "I will explain when we get there" I answered, Blake nodded back then we drove of to my house.

After 10 minutes we arrived at my house and I ran inside and up to Lilacs bedroom, and as soon as I entered, I called for Grandma. She then soon appeared, "Willow?" she asked, "Grandma, where is Lilac?" I demanded, "With us" she answered, "So. She's dead?" I ask with tears rolling down my face, "No, she is nearly though" she told me, "What can I do?" I ask desperately, "Nothing, there is nothing you can do, her magic was practically drained, and that bit a power left, is not enough, and with what she went through, it is harder, she's too weak" Grandma explained, but at that moment, I had an idea. "Bye grandma" I say before making her leave. I turned around and saw Blake also with tears rolling down his face.

"She's. dead?" he choked, "Not yet. But I know what I have to do now" I smile, "I need only you there with me" I explain further, he looked confused, "How old are you again?" he sort of laughed.

After that we went back to the hospital but before I went inside her room I made a spell that will make my parents sleep and my brothers so they can't disturb me. "Okay, let's go" I start, Blake nods, and we walk inside and closed the door them locked it. I sat beside Lilac, a tear rolled down my cheek but I quickly wiped it away, I took out a knife, "Woah, Willow what are you doing!?" Blake asked worried, "Don't worry, it's part of the spell" I quickly say, he nods slowly then sits down,

I then cut my hand, blood starts to pour, "Ow" I whisper, I then reach for Lilac's hand and then cut her hand. I took a breath and grabbed her hand into mine, our blood mixed, I then thought of what I wanted to happen, "Switch, give my power to Lilac" I said in my mind over and over, "Take my power, pass through, enter her" I said, a tingling feeling came on my hand, I then moved my hand away and saw that my cut was healed and so was Lilac's, I smiled, "Please work" I whispered..

Lilac's POV:

I looked down at my hand and saw there was a cut on it, "Grandma?!" I called then she appeared, "What is it dear?" she asked, "My hand? I-it's bleeding?" I stuttered, "It's Willow, she must of done a spell? Or something" she said unsure, "What's going to happen?" I ask, "I don't know" Grandma whispered.. "Switch, give my power to Lilac" a small voice said over and over, it was Willow, "Grandma! She switching out powers?" I screeched, "Isn't that dangerous?" I asked worried, "I don't know, I've never experienced it" she told me, "Take my power, pass through, enter her" Willow's voice said, "Sh-she's giving me her power?" I whispered, "Why?" I asked, but then my hand started to tingle, I looked at it and the cut was healed, The tingling feeling spread through my body, making me glow, "What's happening?!" I cried. Then everything went black.

Chapter 25

Lilac's POV:

I could hear voices, it sounds like there's a lot of struggle, by eyes are too heavy so I can't open them which is annoying because I want to know what the fuss is about. "Doctor what's happening?" a male voice asked, wait a minute I know who's voice that is, "I think she's waking up, I have no idea how this happened" the doctor replied, I had enough I forced my eyes to slowly open, I squinted to adjust to the light, "Oh sorry" the doctor said as he turned the lights down. As soon as my eyes were fully open that's it, everyone jumped up and circled me, "Oh my God!" my mum cried hugging my dad the hugging me, then my dad, then my two brothers and then I saw Blake, "Lilac" he whispered as he pulled me into a tight hug, "I thought I lost you" he cried, "I'm here now" I whisper back. Then I turned to look for Willow but she wasn't here, "Where's Willow?" I asked, "She to the bathroom" my mum replied, "I need her here now" I whisper slowly, "I'll go get her" my mum said then left. She then came back with Willow who looks like she will pass out. "Everyone can you leave, I need to talk to Willow" I ask which everyone nodded to and left.

"Willow" I started, "Why would you do that? It's your power." I ask, "You my sister! I'm not going to let you die!" she replied. "This is not my magic, it's yours and now I can already tell your mortal!" I shook my head, "I don't care, maybe now I can finally be normal" she snapped before leaving. Blake entered the room with a worried expression, "When can I go home?" I asked him, "Today" he whispered, "Then let's go" I say as I stand up slowly but nearly fell so Blake quickly caught me, "Careful, I nearly already lost you once, please don't leave me again" he whispered as he pulled me into a hug. I missed him so much, only now do I realize how much. I cuddled into him more, "I would never leave you" I whisper.

"Come on let's get going" he said as he got me by my waist to help me balance. We started to walk out where we then met up with everyone else, "LEet's go people" I say sluggishly, "But can we please get food on the way, I need proper food" I said acting like I am drunk, Blake chucked, "Yeah okay" he said while kissing the top of my head. I smile at him. After that we got in the car and left then headed to McDonalds, "You really want a McDonalds? Of all the places?" Luca asked, I smiled sheepishly, "Yes, but I need fake meat! I need to eat something rubbish but so good" I protest then folded my arms. Everyone laughed, well except Willow. I sighed.

We all sat in McDonalds, everyone was looking at me, "Lilac" my dad started of, "Dad." I continued, "Why did you do that? You risked your life, you almost died" he asked, I sighed, "I did it to save supernaturals, I know I almost died, it was a sacrifice I was willing to make if it meant to save people like us, I know it was selfish but I would do it all over again" I explained, "Now, when do I go back to school. I'm sorry but I need to put my life back to normal again somehow" I asked randomly, "Well it's Saturday, so Monday?" my mum suggested, I nodded. "I'm sorry everyone. I know I'm making this all so confusing, but I want to forget this all" I apologize, "It's okay, we understand why you would want to, but you are awfully calm" my mum said, "I know, but I was okay so I'm okay now" I explain, everyone nods and continues eating.

"So Willow, your 11th birthday is coming up soon" mum said I looked up in shock, "How long was I in a coma for?!" I ask, "Four months" Blake chocked, I gasp, "Willow's birthday is in a week" Luca quickly explained I just nodded, I then looked at Willow she smiled sadly, I understand now, the reason why she only now just made this decision up was because she wanted me to be alive, and because we made a deal that on her 11th birthday we would then be able to make our deal official, we always made a deal that we would stick together forever no matter what, so we made a spell, but we couldn't use it until Willow turned 11 because only then is her powers fully ready, she wants me to promise to never leave her. But now how can I make this deal?

After we finished we arrived home, "Blake you should probably go, I need to talk to Willow" I ask Blake, I can tell he doesn't want to go but he forced himself to leave, I kissed him goodbye then went to find Willow which I did in her room. "Willow.." I whispered, she looked up at me with tears in her eyes, I then quickly pulled her into a tight hug, "I thought I lost you. Like forever" she whimpered, "I know, I'm sorry, I should never of left you like that, I promise never again" I whisper. "So what happens now?" she asked, "I don't know. I guess I will have to practice using your magic, and as it develops I could transfer some to you as I progress?" I suggested, "No, you can't you need all that magic, you are a powerful witch, you need as much as you can get" she laughed, I just smiled.

"So, you want to know where I went?" I asked while smiling, "What do you mean?" Willow questioned confused, "When I was in a coma, I went somewhere." I smirked, "Where?" and with that I told her everything, from seeing grandma and granddad, the moon goddess, everything..

"Wow, I missed that much aye?" she laughed, "Sort of" I laugh back. "Lilac, you know, now that there are no more hunter's everything is okay, there is nothing for anyone to be afraid of anymore" Willow informed, "I know, yeah so?" I said confused, "No more hiding, we're all okay, everyone is fine. I want you to promise me something now, magic or no magic." Willow said. "Okay what?" I ask, "Live your life, don't worry about me. When I'm old enough I will take care of myself, you don't need to protect me, you and Blake belong together, start a family, don't hold back, I found my mate, although he is a vampire, and will never grow older, I will find someone else and I will be happy. So just promise me that" Willow said, I looked shocked, well obviously, I was about to disagree, "Please" Willow begged, "Fine, but no matter what I will help you, not as much but your my sister, I'm never going to abandon you" I smirk, "I know" Willow laughed. "So now my dear sister Willow, it's time to get our lives back on track" I said making us both laugh.

Chapter 26

It's been a week and now Willow's birthday, it has also been quite normal at school so far, everything seems to be going well, mine and Blake's relationship has intensified, he never really leaves my side and we have fully mates so he has now marked me, also he has made his own pack, with all the wolfs at our school now go to and he is Alpha, making me Luna. A lot has already changed, but it works. My own magic is slowly restoring as well, I learned that no matter what I always have magic of my own, and because Willow gave me hers it has given my magic strength so I am gaining it all back slowly, so I just need to practice. Not everything is perfect though, werewolves and vampires still aren't exactly friends but we're doing okay.

"HAPPY BIRTHDAY!" everyone shouts as Willow walks into the room, she smiles and laughs, as everyone gives her a group hug. The day went by quite fast, we all had a BBQ and just had a fun time for her birthday, and then as it was late at night Willow came into my room, I smile, "Let's try this" I say as we sit on my floor and set up candles around us. Now your most likely wondering what we are going to do, well I am going to try and see Willow's future, to see if she will be a wolf like me, to see if she will be happy, anything and everything, Willow excepted the fact that she is not a witch anymore and she doesn't want to be anymore.

I took her hand and closed my eyes,

I see Willow, older though, maybe like 20 something, there are children and a man, I smile at them all, they're having fun, "Lilac!" Willow screeches, I was taken back, "You see me?" I ask, Willow laughs, "Of course I can, welcome to the future, you were right everything does get better, this is my family, my mate and children. I am also a wolf, I transformed once I found Cole, I joined his pack and we started a life. Before you go back, tell me to take my own advice, I know I'm only 11 but I will understand one day. Tell me, I'm going to make mistakes, there will be bumps on the way but it's nothing we can't handle, Lilac you never left my side, although you had your own family, you were still there. Thank you, I would tell you what happens to you Lilac, but that's a surprise" Willow smiles.

"My little sister Willow, I will see you soon" I smirk before leaving and coming back...

"Did it work?" Willow asked, I smile, "Yes, now let me tell you, you are a wolf, and you are going to be so happy in the future!" I couldn't stop smiling.

Epilogue

2 0 years later....

"Mum! Dad!" my daughter yelled, "Yes?" me and Blake both replied as we stand opposite our daughter, "Can you please tell Jake and Mike to leave me and Maya alone?" Sarah asked, I laughed, "JAKE MIKE!" Blake yelled in his alpha tone, making them both appear fast, "Yes dad?" they both asked, "Stop annoying your sisters" I laugh pulling Blake into a hug, "Sneaky" Jake said to Sarah who was poking her tongue at them both. I smile as Maya appears and flicks both Jake and Mike on the head, "That's for not closing the door" she giggled. "Okay go on out you, but don't be out too late please" I suggest, "Okay bye!" they all said and left. "Oh dear, isn't Jake going to make the perfect Alpha" Blake chuckled, "He is going to be so protective over the girls, along with Mike, they will stick together, we're family" I said like the proud mother I am.

A lot has happened these 20 years, when I turned 18 I fell pregnant with Jake first, then Mike a year later then twins with Sarah and Maya the next year. I'm now 36, Jake has just turned 18, Mike is 17, and Maya and Sarah are both 16. Willow is 30 and has a loving family of her own, so do my brothers. Life was very bumpy but we made it. I'm a fully powerful witch and wolf. Our pack is one the most powerful of all so rogues don't stand a chance.

Today Willow and her family are visiting us, it's been a while since I last saw Willow, so I'm very happy. Willow has three children, a song who is 16, and two daughters, one 13 and one 6. We vowed to stick together no matter what and it has always been this way, and always will.

"Lilac!" Willow shouts from behind me, I turn around and run up to her then hugged her, "It's been a while" I laugh, "A long time" Willow added.